I0563389

Phobos & Deimos

Phobos & Deimos

Two Moons, Two Worlds

John Moehl

RESOURCE *Publications* • Eugene, Oregon

PHOBOS & DEIMOS
Two Moons: Two Worlds

Copyright © 2016 John Moehl. All rights reserved. Except for brief quota-
tions in critical publications or reviews, no part of this book may be repro-
duced in any manner without prior written permission from the publisher.
Write: Permissions, Wipf and Stock Publishers, 199 W. 8th Ave., Suite 3,
Eugene, OR 97401.

Resource Publications
An Imprint of Wipf and Stock Publishers
199 W. 8th Ave., Suite 3
Eugene, OR 97401

www.wipfandstock.com

PAPERBACK ISBN: 978-1-4982-3992-9
HARDCOVER ISBN: 978-1-4982-3994-3
EBOOK ISBN: 978-1-4982-3993-6

Manufactured in the U.S.A.

Contents

Foreword

MARS HAS TWO MOONS: Phobos and Deimos. Like our own moon, always pulling on Planet Earth, creating tides that wash across the globe. My personal world has been pulled by the forces of two different moons. These forces have created two worlds; a bipolar life that is the catalyst for the present work: a collection of short stories.

It is my hope the reader will find in this work a glimpse of lives that may at first seem very foreign; so different as to be pure invention. These are fictional lives and fictional stories; but they are based on real events, real people, and real places. I hope the reader can get of taste of these worlds. I hope I will have been able to communicate to the reader that, even when there are tremendous differences, there are also commonalities. Life is a challenge for all who live it.

Preface

THIS WORK REPRESENTS A series of short fictional writings revolving around my years living and working in various parts of the Africa Region; these years tempered with extended stays in the land of my birth, living in various parts of the United States, from the Northwest to the Southeast. The first contribution attempts to set the stage for this multiple-personality syndrome; the last trying to fix the negative that will yield a lifetime's portrait. Other pieces deal with various aspects of this split personality; observations from a contemplative newcomer on different cultures that link to a universal oneness. Sandwiched between these slices of cerebral whole grain is a filling of episodes depicting various aspects of daily life, the challenges encountered, and the way one must cope with the unexpected. The hoped-for collective thread running through this multi-ethnic goulash is the commonness of humanity. When stripped of all, including our culture and skin color, we are variations of the same organism that is struggling to survive in an often inhospitable world. Most of the tales, modeled after the lifestyles of the 70s and 80s, show evident, and at times striking, differences between life in the United States and Sub-Saharan Africa. What is not so obvious is the humanness we all share.

Acknowledgments

MY EFFORTS HAVE BEEN made possible by my Wife who has helped me see things through the eyes of others. The stories are possible due to her guidance and due to the tremendous generosity of those people across Africa with whom I have had the privilege and pleasure to live and work; people who have given much more than they received. This text would not have been possible without my Wife's further loving support and encouragement nor without the exceptional assistance from Marie, backstopping from her perch in the Tetons.

Acknowledgments

Two Worlds

HAVE YOU EVER BEEN getting out of a boat, when you had one leg still in the boat and the other firmly planted on the dock. The boat begins to drift away and you feel like you are going to be torn apart. This may, in some strange way, partially describe my life where I have two worlds, or at least, like Mars, two moons. One of my moons shines over a "normal" 1950s childhood in the rural Pacific Northwest, when houses and cars were unlocked, drugs came from the drugstore, button-up jeans and a flannel shirt were dress for all occasions, water and air were clean, cars had real chrome metal grills and bumpers, and you could get a "Coke High" at the drive-in after school. This is not to paint too rosy a picture, because I did not particularly like those days when I was living them; and have equally tepid feelings of them when seen through the filter of six decades.

My other moon lights a tropical sky, a postcard photograph of a saucery moon dyed ruby-red by dust, backlighting a skeletal acacia tree on a savannah ridge. This moon casts long shadows that blur fact and fiction, reality and make-believe. The man in this moon at times laughs a belly-wrenching guffaw that mocks man's silliness. The man in this moon cries oily tears for man's desperate condition. This moon illuminates much, but little that is "normal".

However, my moons are not yin and yang, good and evil, light and dark. Each moon has its own gravity and establishes its own atmosphere. Each is its own world. But, as moons, each world is linked to one planet, and part of the same system.

The Super Market

MARKETS ARE NOT ALL the same. Albert had seen pictures in the old newspapers he used for wrapping cloth; pictures of beautiful expansive stores with shiny floors, bright lights, and shelves upon shelves of wonderful merchandize. They called these supermarkets. Well, that may be all well and good, but here in the Central Market, the *marcado*, he knew they, too had a super market.

This was the Big Market and it was truly super with everything anyone could imagine. Whatever you could eat, wear, put in your house, or use on your farm was to be found somewhere in the vast expanse of the market. There were rows upon rows of small market cubicles located around a maze of narrow byways that amounted to footpaths, albeit the pedestrians had to share them with bicycles, mopeds, motorcycles, pushcarts, and even the occasional horse. The shops themselves were a conglomerate of corrugated roofing sheets, wood, and whatever scraps might have been considered useful in constructing some sort of structure to keep out the rain and thieves. Inevitably, regardless of how flimsy the stall, it sported a disproportionately large padlock; a case where size really did not matter because, irrespective of how big, most of these cheap Chinese imports flew open with a good solid rap on their shackle.

The alleyways twisted left and right and back on themselves, the vendors selling dry goods interspersed with small lean-to chop houses and *mimbo* bars. These lanes were more like grooves, worn deep in the soil under the feet of thousands of market-goers. The hard under-surface was overlaid with a smooth ooze of all variety of detritus which took on major proportions in the rainy season. These ruts would be literal streams in the rains, changing to a trickle in the dry season when they transported mostly human by- and waste-products. The combination of these rich liquids and sludge imparted a pungent fragrance to the market that mingled with the tang of cassava, a myriad of special spices, aging fish and meat, along with over-ripening vegetables.

The food-selling portion of the market was located on the Northeast corner of the plaza. Here the goods were sold in long sheds with cement floors and more structured drains. Under the metal-roofed hangers, which burned like ovens in the hot season, the foodstuffs were arranged along wooden tables, the men and women selling the produce sitting behind on a variety of stools and chairs, their children scurrying about. Each vendor had a plastic sheet that corresponded to his or her part of the common table, the fruits or vegetables stacked neatly and artistically in the center of the sheet, loose change carefully secreted under one corner, readily available when needed. The sellers called across the hall to each other, as they hailed customers and screamed after their children while they nursed younger infants or took care of bodily functions perched on pots that took the place of stools.

Outside the greengrocers, in the more open air, there were more bedraggled tables and slabs where the butchers and fish mongers displayed their wares to the buying public and the flies. Vultures and pied crows were strategically sitting on overhangs to avail themselves of any unguarded morsels or jetsam.

In the Southwest corner, sandwiched between the cloth dealers and the taxi stand, was the market's dump heap where all that any one took the time to throw away ended up. Here the stray dogs and rats competed with Daniel, the market fool, for whatever could be ingested, regardless of the ultimate consequences.

Albert loved the market. Not long after sunrise he would arrive in his alley and go to his stall with his *mobylette* which, as soon as he had opened the heavy lock, he would push behind the racks and racks of colorful fabric. When he opened the door the first time each morning, his nose was greeted by the sharp smell of dye from the yards and yards of cloth kept inside. There was rich imported wax cloth from Holland, Indonesia, and England; fluffy denim-colored cloth from Guinea; *plissé* from Mali; *jacquard* and *matelessé* from Sénégal; broadcloth and twill from Belgium; lacy dentelle from Nigeria; flowery textiles from Côte d'Ivoire; rough weaves from Kenya; and, cheap pieces from the local mills. The fabric was all in six- to nine-yard rolls which would be cut based on the customers' needs: most women needing at least six yards to make a full set, *up-and-down*, of a wrapper dress, blouse, and head-tie; men needing only about two yards unless they were planning on sewing the now popular pajama-like *up-and-down* (tops and bottoms) the younger guys sometimes wore.

When he had opened his stall and brought an exceptional selection of his brightest and thickest fabrics to racks near the doors for the scrutiny of passers-by, Albert would take his place on the high bar-type stool just to the side of the doors, cajoling would-be customers and bantering with neighbors and other vendors along the lane.

Soon after he opened up, his helper would arrive: his elder brother's second son. This kid was not the pick of the litter, but he was cheap. Albert's older brother lived in the village and had a full flock of offspring; too many mouths to feed with farms becoming smaller and smaller in size as land was bought up by the big businessmen, all the while, those fields that remained producing less and less as the soils became depleted and fertilizer prices rose. Today, city folk just had to help out their families at home. Albert hoped he was somehow doing some good for those still in the village.

Olivier, Albert's nephew, was in his late teens. He had suffered through his early school years, being too mediocre and disinterested to continue once there was any sort of competition, preferring anything to sitting in a classroom to learn. This was a bit surprising, as his chosen option was to sit all day in a fabric stall. While he was not the brightest, Albert had worked very hard to get him to be able to do mental arithmetic without a calculator, and he was now able to make correct change for customers. Most importantly, Olivier was honest and had a winning smile which helped with reluctant buyers.

Olivier lived in the Boys' Quarters in the back of Albert's house where he was basically free to come and go as he chose. Although

Albert did not pay him much, with his room and board supplied, the loose change in his pocket was readily consumed each night as he went out on the town, frequenting the cheap Off License bars, eating street food, and gallivanting with young hookers.

Even if he often came to work a little late and with more than a little hangover, he was dependable and looked after the shop well when Albert went to lunch or even when he had to go out of town to buy cloth or go back to the village for a funeral or other pressing family matters. Someday Olivier would move on, who knew where? But for the moment he supplied all the assistance Albert needed, and at a bargain price.

Customers would come pretty much throughout the day, with a surge in the early morning and late evening. On a good day he would be able to sell fabric to at least a score of clients, most often women looking for good buys and cheaper cloth. But at the holidays like Ramadan, Christmas and Easter, he would be able to sell the top-of-the-line material for the special occasions to adorn the city's womenfolk and bring due honor to their households as they went forth bedecked in the most lush and colorful fabrics from head to toe.

His selection of fine fabrics was unique and he tended to have repeat customers who knew quality when they saw it. Most were mature women who were willing and able to pay for what they wanted. When he had started in the business he had had numerous young customers, both boys and girls. Today youngsters were more interested in western-style clothes they bought at rock-bottom prices at the *frippery:* that part of the market that sold bulk used clothing that came in bales from Europe and North America.

The Asian businessmen had pretty much monopolized the *frippery* market. They bought clothes given to charities for the poor by the ton and then sold the items by the piece, making huge profits in spite of the low price of the articles. Local shopkeepers had difficult times accessing the global used clothing market. Here, as well as in many other niches, they were unable to compete with their neighbors from Asia.

More and more the markets and consumables were being dominated by outside investors. Bolt fabrics were one of the areas where the local business people were still able to exert some control, although outsiders were lobbying heavily with the local politicians for more and more access, many fearing they would soon dominate all. Albert felt lucky to be in one of the few areas where he considered himself master of his own destiny, or at least his own profit.

Fabric sales, nevertheless, were not the most exciting of lifestyles. Certainly not to what Albert had aspired as a young man. In those heady days of his youth he had thought the world was his, and all was possible. But he, like Olivier, had left school early. He had married and become a husband and father, as Olivier was likely to do in the not too distant future.

As the years piled on, his life took on a familiar, if un-invigorating, routine revolving around, of all things, cloth. Early to bed and early to rise, his shop open seven days a week, except Christmas and Easter, from seven in the morning until seven at night. His days were his alleyway. When he left his stool, after the morning rush he would go to one of the tiny cafés or chop houses for a cup of *Nescafé* and a half baguette. Around mid-day he would return to one of these eateries for a plate of plantains and meat sauce—*condré*—or maize meal with melon seed soup. By the afternoon, after a filling meal, he would fight off the urge for a nap by chewing kola nuts and playing *Ludo* with his fellow fabric sellers; the board game others called Parcheesi. When the government offices closed at five, there would be another small wave of customers who were shopping on their way home. By the time he pushed his *mobylette* back outside, gave Olivier a teeny tip, and snapped the mighty lock shut, it was already well after dark. He part peddled, part road the thirty minutes back to his small home *au quartier* in the northern suburbs of this mid-sized city that served as the administrative and commercial core of the whole province.

Each evening, when he came through the door into his parlor, lit by a hissing gas lantern, he felt like a traveler reaching his destination. The lamp cast shadows and created a silky light that was like looking through one of his gossamer fabrics. The smells of kerosene, wood smoke, and hot palm oil seemed to blend into a homey cologne. He would greet his family, play a bit with his children, eat a hardy meal surrounded by the love of his family, and then fall on his bed and dream of his youth, running carefree across the plains, and smelling the coming rain.

The next day, come rain or shine, he would be back on his stool, anxious to bargain over the best waxes or the cheapest poplin. All was well with the world when Albert was at his shop.

Then one day he came to open his doors to find a wrinkled sheet of paper crudely stuck to his doors with common white paste. What was this epistle? There, nearly hidden by the city, commune, and Ministry of Finance stamps were the few words that would change Albert's life: Notice to Shop Owners—effective immediately the Central Market will be relocated to the old parade field; market space and licenses to be allocated on a first-come-first-serve basis to those vendors who present a written demand, proof of tax payment, and a deposit of two-hundred-thousand francs.

This was the knell of doom. The rumors have been flying about the Mayor's intentions. It was now clear. All the impossible was soon seen as possible, as Albert confirmed the situation with adjacent shopkeepers. The current market plaza would be leveled and converted into a taxi park and bus station, the Mayor holding all the concessions for fuel and food for the businesses supplying the transporters and their travelers. What's more, the Mayor had already sold all the licenses for the new market to his political cronies, family, folks from his village, and high-paying Asians. This meant that the only way the current businessmen could continue in the new market would be by sub-contracting with the new license holders, paying as much as ten times the price to be able to open a new stall; a sum most would not make in a year. The long and short of it was that they were all shut down.

The super market was no more and the super marketers were adrift. Each was pushed and pulled by the tides and winds of their own sphere; Albert feeling as though he was dashed on the rocks and pummeled by the surf. He managed to keep his stall open for another two weeks before the bulldozers came, liquidating as much of his lovely stock as possible before he removed his remaining inventory to his house, putting piles of bolts in the corner of his room and under the bed.

Once the market was razed, Albert felt as empty as the old market plaza. He had no clue of what to do now. He had little or no chance to get a license for a stall in the new a market. He could not go back to the village. The extended family's resources were already over-subscribed. Furthermore, he owned his home and had children in school here in the city. He had no special skills and would be most reluctant to become someone's Olivier—a simple store helper. How could he pay his bills, keep food on the table, and keep his kids in school?

When the new market had been built, Albert went to see if by any means he could find a way to have a stall. What he found was an aberrant structure in no way resembling a super market; rather a maze of prefabricated interlinked blockhouses with no personality and critically no ventilation. Furthermore, there was absolutely no chance for him to get a shop. Not only could he not get in, but all his former competitors also found themselves on the outside, the new market's fabric sales completely under the thumbs of Asian businessmen who sold only cloth from their part of the world. There were no more rich batiks or waxes, no woven *kente* or colorful *kangas*; there was only blasé poor quality machine-made material that was not suitable for a curtain, let alone a fine set of clothes for Christmas.

Olivier was luckier. His experience, but lack of ambition, made him the perfect gofer for the new cloth sellers and he had quickly found a new employer. He had wanted to keep on living with Albert, but this was plainly impossible and he had had to find a room to rent somewhere in the *quartier* which almost made his balance sheet negative from the onset.

Albert's wife was full of suggestions. What of this, what of that? Why not try this? Did you ever think of . . . ? While he did try to examine the opportunities and take the advice from his wife, or anyone else who was thoughtful enough to offer it, he found no open roads. He was at a dead end and did not know how to turn around.

If he had more money, he would have become a drunk; killing the pain with *kaikai*, *arki*, or any home distillate that would bring numbness to his troubled brain. If he had been able, he might have even killed himself; but this too was something he did not even know how to set about. So he worried and worried and worried.

Every day he walked about town looking for some possible chance, some way to keep his head above water. He was lost.

The pressure built and he continued his fruitless pursuit of another life. Then, one day as he walked home after yet another unsuccessful pilgrimage around town, he saw a flash of light, felt a snap like a branch breaking in the wind, and then felt nothing.

He awoke in a dirty bunk in a dirty ward in the Central Hospital, seeing his wife sitting on the dirty floor next to his foul bed. He tried to ask her what had happened but nothing seemed to work. He moved his lips, or at least thought he did, but there was no sound, or no sound he could hear. He was confused and afraid.

When is wife became aware of his wakefulness, she came close and moved her lips in his face but he heard nothing. She saw his big, fear-filled eyes and realized serious damage had been done. She tried to make gestures for him to calm down; to reassure him that she would do what needed to be done, although she had no idea of what could or should be done.

She tried valiantly to do something, anything. She ran to the Matron's desk and begged someone to come and help. She grabbed nurses, doctors, and hospital aids by their sleeves and tried to drag them to her husband's bedside. She screamed and she pleaded, but all she received were patronizing shrugs and a few indifferent words soliciting patience. Patience. She had been patient. She had waited for hours for someone to come to her husband. No one had come and no one came. Patience. There was no more patience. There was nothing.

Totally exhausted, she returned to the ward and slumped by the bed. What had happened with their life? What would become of their life?

Through some sort of distorted haze like gossamer cloth, Albert sensed more than saw his wife. Somehow he felt her love. And then he took her by the hand and led her into the new super market with rows and rows of fabric dealers selling the finest materials. He saw her dressed in a magnificent English wax, with her head-tie high and haughty. Life was good.

Afflictions of Man

His Mother had warned him: "don't get sick". As a small boy Henri had been worried about getting sick. Like many of the children in the village, he was slight of build and, when he saw pictures of European kids in the old newspapers wrapping the meat from the market, he felt like he was really so puny that the risk of illness was all too real. This is not to say he was a blooming hypochondriac, forever watching where he stepped, what he ate, or with whom he associated; his Aunt was well enough obsessed with these characteristics for the whole family. No, he was a regular child who climbed trees, swam in the creek, and chased lizards when he was not in school or the fields. But, like the cicada buzzing on a hot afternoon, his Mother's words were a tiny but omnipresent hum in his mind.

As the years passed, the hum dulled to the point he did not notice it unless he really listened for it. Nothing had happened to amplify the warning. In spite of his sparse frame, he had shown himself to be resilient. He had overcome several bouts with malaria and diarrhea; weakened but more resistant afterward.

This was fortunate because, as his Mother had known so well, had he had serious health problems, the only option would have been the village dispensary or the local healer. The former was a disheveled building with a tiny cadre of disheveled staff; the building and the staff long forgotten by the provincial health authorities. The head nurse was a native from the village who had worked in the city decades ago, with who-knows-what training. She had one assistant and one cleaner, both with equal education and skill. If the clinic received any supplies, and it rarely did, these were bandages, antiseptic, and aspirin.

The village healer was attributed with several miraculous healings and was reputed to have an impressive knowledge of the use of local plants, herbs, and minerals to heal man's afflictions, as well as more than a passing acquaintance with the darker side of traditional healing methods. Any hesitancy, however, in seeking treatment from this gentleman would not be due to skepticism as to the efficacy of the treatments, but rather due to the cost of receiving them. The good shaman enjoined equally good remuneration for his services, which exceeded the means of his family in all cases save those of very noticeable life-threatening conditions; certainly not simple affairs like malaria or diarrhea.

Henri recalled his Aunt had found a third alternative, but it remained to be seen if this was truly an option for health. On her regular visits to the district Big Market she would come back with a small plastic bag filled with pills and capsules of the colors of the rainbow. Her baggy was a rather good sub-sample of the bags of pharmaceuticals sold by young boys in the taxi park. They would reach in and randomly pull out a tablet or ampule, proudly proclaiming its powers at fighting fever, chills, and the flux. Henri's Aunt had swallowed all variety of concoctions provided by the taxi park boys. Loudly praising their effectiveness until another strange *maladie* found a home in her scraggly body.

With the passing of his youth, having completed his first five years of primary school and adding some meat to his bones, Henri took a taxi to the nearest city to find employment and a more invigorating lifestyle.

In surprisingly short time, perhaps due to his enthusiasm and winning smile, he found a job as a *moto-boy* with a local trucker. While being a driver's gofer did not pay well, it had several advantages. The truck was on the road nearly constantly, meaning he did not have to worry about accommodation in the city; he slept under the truck on his mat, even when in town. More importantly, he was a *de facto* apprentice driver, most truckers starting as *moto-boys*, learning the trade, and making the contacts.

Henri passed his weeks and months in the hot cab of the Mercedes truck, the howling of the engine completely drowning out the hum in his mind. He would change the flats and change the oil. He would clean the cab and the windscreen. He would seek men, looking for a few francs, to help him load and unload the cargo ranging from coffee and cement to cattle and telephone poles.

The vagabond lifestyle excluded his establishing close friendships and even his finding a candidate for a wife. His main social distractions came at truck-stops where he would move about with the other *moto-boys* his age, spending a few francs for roasted meat or plantains, having some cups of *arki*, the cheap locally distilled high-octane alcohol, or an occasional beer. As he grew older and his hormones began to take more control, he began also to include a stop at any of the many bordellos for a "quickie" with an older hooker; all a poor *moto-boy* could afford.

Henri's life had now taken a new routine, distant and removed from the village and its bucolic life. He rarely went home. It was not that he felt it beneath him, far from it. However, when someone went back to the village from the city, they had to go back with gifts and offerings for the family; and the extended family in the village was large. The pittance paid a *moto-boy* would not allow him to return home often with the largess he felt he needed to compensate for those youthful years growing up which had been truly joyous.

He managed to get home for either Christmas or Easter, and would generally find himself there for at least one additional visit a year, for the important wedding or funeral; the later becoming more and more frequent as the years passed.

His life now was concentrated in the hot, shaking cab of the truck with the perfume of sweat mixed with diesel. The newness of this wore off as the rigors took their toll. Constant noise and vibration combined with sleeping on the cold, often wet ground, added to poor diet began to accelerate the aging process and at thirty-five, as he was now looking for a new job as a driver, he looked nearly twice his age.

Fortunately, his smile had not aged with his body and he had been able to make some very promising contacts that seemed highly likely to lead to a driver position with the corresponding increase in salary; nearly a ten-fold gain to be anticipated. Only the final discussions remained, and it seemed likely he would soon be behind the wheel of his own rig, with his own *moto-boy* to boss about.

As the details were being sorted out, he continued to suffer in what he now saw as a beat-up carcass of a lorry compared to what he hoped would be his new charge. He begrudgingly spread his mat under the chassis every night, thinking of the day in the not too distant future when he might be able to get a room of his own with a real bed and maybe even running water and electricity, if he were very, very lucky.

He sullenly unloaded the sacks and bails, regretting the continuous pain in his lower back and longing to feel the gearshift of a big rig in his hand, instead of the wheelbarrow handle to which he was harnessed to unload a mountain of sand. He was a short-timer now and he felt it.

When all the arrangements had been made and he had given his current boss his notice, the day came when he was ready to make his last run as a *moto-boy*. This final venture involved going to the port city to pick up a load of soap from the factory. On the outward leg, they would pick up vegetables along the road to sell in the port and then return the next day with boxes and boxes of block soap.

All went as planned and they slowly climbed the hills from the coastal plain to the highland savannah when it happened. The brakes went out on a down-hill-bound truck loaded with beer from the nearby brewery. The beer truck teetered to the left and to the right before it careened head-on into the cab of Henri's truck. The momentum from the final impact shifted the beer crates to the front, crashing through the wall separating the bed and the cab, mincing the brewery truck's driver and *moto-boy* in a flurry of broken glass. This same impact threw Henri's boss through the windscreen and on to the pulp that had been the inhabitants of the beer truck's cab. Henri was saved from this same fate by the fact that his leg was wedged between the seat and the door, preventing him from becoming air-born at the time of the concussion.

Henri awoke, immediately aware of the sting of antiseptic in his eyes and nose and the ring of crying in his ears. As luck would

have it, if one could even use the term in the context of such a gro-
tesque accident, the lorries had collided not ten kilometers from a
mission hospital.

The main road to the port was well-travelled and the accident
itself was witnessed by many people in many vehicles; passenger
cars, taxis, buses, trucks. The taxi that had been immediately behind Henri's truck as it climbed the hill, narrowly missed smash-
ing into the back of the truck as the driver hit the brakes.

The taxi driver was a big man with great strength, both physical and emotional. He first pulled his vehicle well away from the
trucks for fear of fire and then offloaded all his passengers as he
went to inspect the terrible wreckage. As the first on the scene,
he saw Henri hanging out of the space where the windscreen had
once been. When he opened the passenger door he saw Henri's
horribly mangled leg, the leg that had prevented him from being
immediately killed, but which was now a twisted stick of sinew
and macerated flesh. The leg was, in fact, so loosely connected to
the rest of the body that the taxi driver could quite easily turn the
booted foot to dislodge it and carefully remove Henri's body from
the dash.

He carried the limp form to his taxi and spread it out on the
back seat before dashing at top speed to the mission hospital. He
slid to a stop at the hospital entrance, gently lifting Henri into his
arms and carrying him to the reception as he screamed for a doctor and urgent help.

His screams were met with supreme indifference as the
matron averted her eyes from the mutilated limb and asked the
taxi-man for the patient's hospital card. There was, of course, no
card and there was also no running to help; no gurney, no doctor,
not even a nurse, only the stoic matron. The taxi-man called her
a nincompoop in six languages and yelled for help at the top of
his lungs. When there was still no reaction, he charged into the
interior of the hospital, Henri in his arms, barging into each room
until he finally found someone in a white coat and stethoscope,
someone at whom he too yelled to come and save this poor man's
life. The grit in the driver's voice seemed to stir the stethoscope

man to life; his eyes became less glazed and he actually took in the full gravity of the circumstances. Like someone coming out of a dream, he half led, half pushed the driver into a sordid operating room, whereupon he shoved the driver out as he too began yelling for nurses, instruments, and medications.

Henri was aware of none of this and the taxi-man had long since gone back to his passengers. Henri had practically no memory of anything. In the deep recesses of his mind, where the cicada had stayed, he seemed to recall a man in a white coat saying, "I hope you are a hero". And then, there was blackness.

The blackness was now replaced by fuzzy grey as Henri looked about. He was in a metal bed, apparently with springs and a mattress underneath him, almost like the bed he had dreamed of getting once he had his own truck. The grubby sheets were covered with a grey, frayed blanket that matched the gun-metal grey walls, painted with oil paint that could be scrubbed from all the afflictions that lived in the ward. The ceiling had apparently been white but was now fly-specked, dusty, and grey. The beds in the ward next to his were occupied by people who looked grey. His world was grey.

With great difficulty he raised his head slightly, quickly noting only one hump under his blanket. Although he could clearly feel his right foot, when he painfully moved his hand to where his right thigh should be, there was nothing. He had lost his leg.

The drugs, the shock, and the fatigue blissfully took him away from the grayness into the cloudless skies of his mind where the cicadas were silent and the air smelt of fresh fallen rain.

When he awoke again he found his Mother sleeping on a mat next to his bed; next to her a worn vinyl bag and some chipped enamel pots. As was typical of that place and time, hospitals provided medical care, such as it was, and, if possible, a roof over the patient's head. All else was up to the *malade* (the sufferer) and the family. Families fed, bathed, and sometimes changed bandages for their loved ones.

Henri's ward was like a small village with each bed having its own "household", sometimes including children and the aged.

The caregivers, generally mothers, wives, or sisters, prepared food on the open hearths outside the compound. They assisted their family members to the latrines in the back. They bathed them with sponge baths if they were too weak, or in small mat-covered spaces near the latrines if the patients had the strength to stand for a dousing of cold and often defiled water. They would hound the nurses and nurses aids, cajoling or even bribing them to make sure their family member had some modicum of care.

This task was no easy matter for the families. The "nurses", many of whom had no real formal training, wore white smocks that covered smart dresses ballooning above shiny high-heeled shoes. They looked and acted more like someone out on the town than someone set at healing the afflicted. These sisters of mercy would haughtily pass the ill with their noses in the air, paying no mind to empty IVs, soiled bandages, and even the unfortunate women in labor who could no longer wait their turn in the queue, but gave birth in crowded and filthy corridors. The same corridors down which the nurses glided.

So it was that Henri's Mother set about her task of shepherding her son to better health. Truly he could never again aspire to good health, but he was lucky to be alive. He could regain his strength and be strong enough to leave this place of sadness on his one good leg. She cooked and bathed. She coaxed and soothed. She even learned to effectively spend the few coins she had to ensure her son received the medications actually prescribed, as the staff were prone to sell real medications on a gravely undersupplied black market, giving the patients whatever they found, regardless of the implications.

Like the proverb, little by little a bird makes its nest, little by little Henri regained his physical strength, if not his mental resilience. With his Mother's help he began to hobble around the ward on crutches; first for a few minutes a day and ultimately for hours at a time. While his afflictions were terrible and life-changing, they were not terminal like so many others in the ward. During the weeks it took for him to be able to reach an acceptable level of hopping with crutches, scores of men and women had come and gone from the ward. Many going to the grave and not back to the village.

The day came when Henri and his Mother took a taxi back to their village, where he was warmly welcomed by all. After the initial fires of welcome for the nearly-dead son of the community waned, Henri exercised and practiced until he was very proficient at getting around and taking care of himself. But, as good as he got, he was not able to do man's work. He could not go to the fields, build a house, or even tend the goats. He could sit in the sun with the elders, as they warmed themselves and commiserated. And sit he did, for hours and days on end. These tedious periods were only made bearable by the fact that he was able to learn a great deal from the aged as they talked of times gone by, tradition, mystery, and the way things were.

His mind absorbed the history and culture, the knowledge a salve for his mind almost as though it were rubbed on the nub where his leg should have been. He listened and learned. He questioned and understood. Quite by chance, he became the memory of his community; the repository for its culture and past. These mental stretches and calisthenics completed the healing process and, after months sitting on a bamboo stool in the sun, he was finally ready to accept himself as he was and no longer as he had been.

However, as his mind began to tune into his new reality, he realized he could not stay forever in the village. He was a burden to his family. While he now had a status of prominence because of his brush with death and, more recently, because of his great understanding of the village's history, he was an additional mouth to feed—a mouth connected to a body that made no productive contribution.

The following dry season, after good rains and the signs that the harvest would be good, Henri decided to go back to the city and see what he could do for himself; his selfless proclamations reinforced by feelings that he really needed to get back to the real world before he came totally imbedded in the village.

On the day of his departure, his Mother accompanied him to nearby main road where he flagged down a taxi to start his travels back to the past. His Mother carried his small vinyl satchel as he hobbled along beside her. She had no idea of what would now become of her son. She only knew this was another of those thresholds from which there was no going back. Whatever would happen, good or bad, barring a catastrophe such as his past accident, Henri had left.

When the driver had thrown his bag and crutches on the luggage rack, Henri pushed and was pushed into a seat in the back of the minibus. As the taxi pulled back onto the road, he looked back through the dust-covered window at his Mother standing lonely on the red laterite shoulder, and he too wondered what was in store? And, he too knew he was not likely to come back, at least not to stay.

After a rough-and-tumble trip, made all the more rough-and-tumble due to his handicap, he arrived back in the city in early evening after most of the traffic had subsided and the roll through the suburbs and slums was reasonably quick and still lit by a nearly setting sun.

The city seemed to have changed greatly during his absence; new buildings, new roads, and whole new neighborhoods. But when he finally set his good leg on the ground, he found that really nothing had changed. It was the same old city with the same old problems and the same old people. With his bag slung across his back and his weight on his crutches, he hopped out of the taxi park, but had no idea of where to go.

He still had his winning smile and a good knowledge of the by-ways of town. So, he migrated back to his old haunts, shuffled past the lorry park where he had spent many, many hours; moving past the chop houses now bustling with evening customers and, almost by chance, found himself at the Catholic Mission where, in other times, he had never set foot—or at those occasions, feet. Given the late hour and his lost state, both mentally and socially, this now seemed like he right place to put his foot and he hopped up the stars of the priory and rang the bell.

The brothers at the mission were not overly apt to accept uninvited guests, although they were called the Brothers of Charity.

They felt, and perhaps rightfully so, that, once the door was opened, they would be overrun. There would be no turning back the flood nor any way to keep all the souls that would come to them for help.

Nevertheless, whether it was seeing the beaming smile or the missing leg, the elderly brother who opened the door did not drive Henri away as he had done to so many so often, but, after astutely assessing his needs, offered him a mattress in the workers' quarters that came with a plate of porridge to be repaid by helping in the kitchen.

Henri managed to stay for few weeks at the mission to figuratively "get his feet under himself". However, the brothers made it clear from the onset that this was not a limitless gesture, for which they would pay an endless price. This was a very special and unique display of compassion for a young man who was willing to work hard in spite of his infirmity.

So it was that Henri had by chance arranged for himself a bit of a breathing space to try and see how a man with one leg could survive in the city; having been unable to survive mentally in the village. He had had to promise the brothers that he would work in the kitchen three times a day to pay for his humble board and room, but he still had quite some time to hobble around the city to see what his options were. He went back to the lorry and taxi parks, to the big market and the smaller trading centers, to the major shopping area, and several hotels, restaurants, and even construction sites.

His locomotion by crutches had greatly developed his torso and Henri had tremendous strength in his arms that he thought could perhaps be used in some way or other: washing, ironing, cooking, cleaning, almost anything that did not require one to move around very much. He also could read and had some basic arithmetic; skills which, he had hoped, might be a consideration to get a job as a clerk or some other type of simple desk work. However, as his stay with the brothers came to an end, he was no closer than when he started to finding a way to stay alive in the city.

In his searches about town, he would frequently pass in front of the main grocery stores and pharmacies frequented by the town's elite; the expatriates, high-level functionaries, and business-men. Stuck outside the entrances and exits from these establish-ments were coveys of the handicapped with all shape and form of deformity and incapacity. They were amassed nearly like flies on offal; an amorphous mass of humanity that had, in fact, a hidden structure. There was a leadership structure and a pecking order to determine who actually sat, squatted, or lay in the prime spots where the targets had to literally stumble over the oppressed, and hence they were more likely to throw some coins at them, just to get out of the way. It was even rumored that the chiefs of these tribes of the forgotten were so rich some were brought to their begging stations by chauffeured Mercedes limousines.

Every time Henri passed these spots, he saw himself as one of those thrusting a begging bowl or leprosy-ridden hand in the faces of the wealthy, awaiting their crumbs, while under the thumb of the beggars' chief, who would extort a toll on every penny scratched from the scarred pavement upon which they perched. There was no way he could become one of them, but there appeared to be few options.

His mind and his situation were in such a great state of flux and uncertainty that he swallowed what little pride he had left and begged the brothers to let him stay a few more months. Perhaps it was pity or perhaps it was really needing an extra pair of hands in the kitchen, but Henri got his reprieve and was given, with the beneficence of those with the luxury of having more than they needed, the exceptional gift of six more months at the mission. Henri was late to learn that this benevolence was much more prac-tical management than empathy for his predicament. It was now approaching Christmas, a most busy time for the mission. More-over, several of the older brothers would be returning to Europe in summer when the vacation season started; the mission needed short-term help and the devil you knew was the lowest risk.

Through the Holidays Henri had great hopes that the festive time of man loving man would translate into his chance for some means to become self-sufficient and start a new life on his own, if not on his own two feet. But, alas the new year arrived with no change. Easter came and went as Henri came and went around town, leaving no stone unturned, looking everywhere but finding an opportunity nowhere.

On his way back to the mission from the suburbs where he had been job hunting, he noticed his bus surrounded by vendors as it waited at the traffic light. Like this light, another light went off in his head. He saw people in wheelchairs and on crutches selling chewing gum, *bon-bons*, matches, and soap along with the horde of young children and women. This group had been so much a part of the scenery that he had not seen it; the trees for the forest syndrome. These people seemingly were able to make a living by selling the commonest of items to an imprisoned audience of customers; passengers and drivers of motor vehicles having no change to avoid the deluge of vendors, and many finding this a convenient time to purchase the small snacks and items they would have ordinarily bought at roadside kiosks.

Back in the mission kitchen, he asked the other workers what they knew about the sellers in the go-slow; those who benefited most from the traffic lights and jams around the city. He learned the group moved up and down the main thoroughfares; hitting incoming avenues in the morning when traffic was heading into the city, and the main arteries going out when the business day closed. This group, too, had its chiefs and structures, but there was not the stigma of being a beggar at the pharmacy.

Overlords bought the small items sold on the streets in bulk and then resold them to those who attacked the cars and buses. These entrepreneurs not only made a profit on the re-sales to the street vendors, but also required a small percentage off the top. Nevertheless, and surprisingly to Henri, the vendors were able to do quite all right. This was why there were so many children and women. They could make more money selling toilet rolls or batteries under the unforgiving sun and in the dangerous traffic than they could make if they had stayed in the village. They could actually make a living doing this.

Henri now had a plan. He spent his time among the street vendors until he had made friends with several. Slowly he was able to get the needed details and contacts, to have a supplier, and a space to share with the others with whom he shared the street. The summer came and Henri finally left the mission with no real sorrow. He now had a place to go, a job to do, somewhere to sleep, and even the possibility of saving a few coins to take back to the village next Christmas.

As he deftly dodged cars when the lights changed or the jams became unplugged, the cicadas sang again and he remembered his Mother's words. He would not get sick. He would get well.

The Path of Life

SHE WAS CALLED JOSE, short for Josepha. She was eleven and in primary school. She went to school in Bankim, about twenty-five kilometers from her home village of Bankop. She would have liked to stay at home and go to school there, but her family was just too big; she had six sisters and seven brothers. There was no way her Mother and Father could feed a crew that large. Fortunately, the extended family system offered options and she was living with her Mother's childless younger sister—Aunt Ndija.

In many ways this move to her Aunt's house was a blessing in disguise. Although she missed her family and her home terribly, school in the mid-size city of Bankim was much better than that in the village. No self-respecting teacher wanted to live in the village with no electricity, running water, or health center. The village teachers tended to be either semi-retired educators who had returned to the village from the city or else they were the real failures who couldn't find a job anywhere else. If you weren't lucky, you could end up with a village grade school teacher who was a drunk or child molester, or both.

Ndija and her husband Amidou were truly wonderful people. They lived on a small hill about three kilometers north-west of the market, on the town's outskirts. They were far enough out of town where they could have a small farm around the house. They had a stand of plantains as well as mixed crop fields; depending on the season, maize, cassava, yams, groundnuts, or beans. They also had a small hen house with ten hens and a rooster; these birds providing enough eggs for their own needs plus a few extra for sale in the market.

The house itself was small, made of mud blocks with a cement and sand plaster and a tin roof over a bamboo celling. There was a large living-dining room with big wooden double doors as well as three sets of large shuttered windows. There was one large bedroom and three smaller ones; each of the smaller bedrooms occupied by a girl from one of Ndija's brothers or sisters. This was a real luxury for the girls, for they surely would not be able to have a room to themselves if they had stayed at home.

The house was spotless. The floor and some of the walls and cupboards were polished to a high shine with the sap of a local shrub. The windows had curtains, the end tables were doily-covered. The salon, whose floor was covered with a colorful woven reed mat, had a comfortable settee and sofa, along with a variety of other chairs and stools. There was a large and well organized detached kitchen along with a bathroom and privy in the back of the compound.

Although the town had both electricity and running water, they were far enough out not to be able to have either service. However, the house had a very effective cistern system which supplied stored rainwater throughout the year. There were also hurricane lamps on high stands that illuminated the house very well, even in the darkest night.

In addition to Jose, there were her older cousins Colette and Mary. Colette was the second daughter of Jose's Mother's big brother and Mary was the third daughter of her Mother's eldest sister, the first born of the family. Collette was in secondary school, *college*, while Mary was an apprentice for a local *couturier*.

Jose was in the final years of her primary school education, going to school at the *Mission Catholique* on the other side of the market, about a forty-five-minute walk from Ndija's home. She would take a short cut, a path that followed a small stream down the hill and passed by the slaughterhouse before joining the main dirt road just half a kilometer from the market.

In general, she loved her walk along the path. Although she would close her eyes and sometimes even plug her ears when she walked by the slaughterhouse, and pretended not to see the red rivulet that came from there to join the stream, her perambulations up and down the path were highlights of the day. School was fine and she was an average student, albeit all told her she was above average when it came to smarts. But school was boring. School was a job that had to be done. School was claustrophobic. The boys pestered her, the girls often teased her because she was already striking at such a young age. The teachers leered and imagined but, thankfully, kept their hands off. School was to be tolerated but was certainly not enjoyed.

In fact, it was more her sense of obligation to her family and not the idea of getting an education that kept her in school. Neither her Mother nor Father had gone to school and they both regretted this shortcoming. Her parents made great sacrifices to help with her upkeep at Ndija's and she could not let them down. So each day she walked up and down the path, the trip much more pleasant than the destination.

When she would leave home, she would start her trip in the fields surrounding the town and would join the path already populated by women going early to the fields to weed a maize patch or dig a coco yam for the evening meal. The women would have a baby strapped to their back, a hoe hooked over their shoulder, and a small basket with some provisions balanced skillfully on their head. She would meet men and women going the other way, to further away farms or going home with bundles of wood for cooking the morning meal. There would also be other children going to school as well as people going to the market to open stalls or shop for necessities. Most often people moved along the path in small groups of two or three, chatting and laughing, but always greeting all they met. Different groups would even keep up animated conversations amongst themselves as they moved along the trail. The rich, resonant voices were morning melodies that accompanied the crowing of the roosters and the singing of birds in the surrounding eucalyptus plantations.

As they got closer to town the number of people going to farms decreased while the numbers going to school and market swelled. There were people on bicycles, with a few better-off shop keepers riding motorcycles or *mobylettes* along the narrow by-way. All seemed in a hurry, but none were in so much of a hurry not to be able to greet and even stop to chat about the night's rain storm or the new District Officer's wife.

As the town got closer, the path widened and there were more pedestrians and more produce. There were small children pushing hand-crafted wooden scooters, there were men pushing wheelbarrows with fertilizer, there were boys with rented *pousse-pousses,* taking these handcarts to market to look for customers. There were men and women with great bundles on their heads, taking their harvests and wares to market, while others drove small flocks of sheep or goats and the occasional pig. Sometimes there were even nomadic *Foulanis* with a small herd of cattle.

When the slaughterhouse was in sight, the path was nearly a lane, filled to the brim with all sorts of people and contraptions. Then, as it joined the main road it became a true flood of humanity. It seemed as though everyone from the town and the surrounding district was on the road going somewhere to do something important, moving with great purpose, but always having the time to meet and greet.

At this stage, Jose imagined herself as a canoe floating in a river of the masses. She went with the flow and absorbed the gaiety and congeniality. There was great excitement and joy in the air. In the dry season there were so many people that they raised little clouds of dust and in the rainy season they were so numerous that you could hear the mud gush from under their feet. She floated in this river until it deposited her at the school.

There, almost like a dog shaking off the rain, she had to let go of the high-energy outside world and refocus on reading, writing, and arithmetic. This was like penance for the pleasure of the journey to school and payment for the similar pleasures to be enjoyed on the return trip.

Jose was not just a spectator in these daily rituals. She was definitely an actor. She would be the first to greet and knew by name many of those she encountered, including often knowing enough to ask about a family member or friend. There was a subset of those with whom she shared the path for whom she would always stop, even if only for a minute, to talk and share a smile. She would also joyously hail all those who inhabited the margins of the path, with the exception of those at the slaughterhouse.

She would wave and greet the shopkeepers, the bar tenders, the cafe servers, the office workers, and the laborers. She felt she was one of them or they were one of hers. In some ill-defined way, they were all one. Not all one because they shared the path. Not one because they shared the town. Not even one because were, to a large part, the same ethnic group. It was not this analytical. She simply and purely felt they were all one and should respect, if not love, each other as being part of the one.

Years later Jose remembered the path. The years had been kind to her but they had inevitably changed her. The harmony was no more. With great sadness she had learned that the naivety of youth was all too sweet, if not too unreal. Were that we were all really one. What a difference that would make. But, most unfortunately, a smile along the path is not proof of a good heart. People are people, as she had painfully learned. She so wished she could walk that path again.

She fondly recalled how meticulously Ndija had taught her and the other girls, prepared them all for the path. Ndija had always been insistent: "look your best and do your best". Jose, that young girl happily walking to school, had not been someone who had just jumped out of bed and joined the world. She had been someone who had prepared each and every day for the path as carefully guided by Ndija. Clean body and clean, if patched and mended, clothes. Fresh and carefully tied scarf. Just the slightest touch of *Foulani* makeup. An artistic touch of pencil around the eyes. Some oil or cream on the skin. This had not been preening. This had not been *haute culture* or *beau ideal*. This had not been elegance or vanity. This had been simply the right way to do things. Self-respect and family honor dictated that you took time to look acceptable as you joined the path and the community. When Jose had finished her preparation for her daily trek she would receive an inspection by Ndija and a final assessment by Amidu before going out; thereby representing them, as it should be, as much as herself.

As she moved from childhood to adulthood, the years had painfully taught that, sadly, there was no "one". The small and petty exerted forces that countered what should have been the over-arching good. The smile could be painted and the milk of human kindness could sour. Reality was, in fact, all too real. Nonetheless, irrespective of the painfulness of seeing things for what they were, and not what they could have been, there was still another "one". She wistfully knew now that this was not the "one" of humanity. But, there was the "one" of self. The "one" that Ndija had groomed and guided. She now knew she could put on her makeup and scarf and hold her head high as she walked down the path. Even if it was not that path of so long ago.

The Game

THE VILLAGE WAS LOCATED on the flood plain nourished by a massive river that had brought the ancestors to this forested delta. By some accounts, life had changed relatively little over the years and the region remained isolated and under-developed. Simon, of course, could not attest to how it would have been to live here a hundred years ago, but he knew it was tough to live here today. Many things had come and gone, but only the river remained and set the pace of life for all. Villagers were baptized with the river's waters and interred in watery graves on its shores. Between these two milestones, they structured their lives around the river's floods and droughts, knowing the river alone was sure and would care for them when all else failed.

The river was like a great sleeping boa; its color nearly the same, mottled shades of brown, the snake's coloration part of its natural camouflage, the river's a result of tons and tons of silt it carried from the hinterland. The river, like the snake, often moved deceptively slowly, but could react with amazing speed, sucking the unsuspecting into its murky waters never to surface again in this world.

The river was the heart of daily life. It was the main means of communication and transport. It provided the abundant fishes that adorned family plates. Its silt enriched the riverside gardens of cassava and yams. Its encompassing forests provided game for the pot and materials for the home and the hearth as well as a broad array of medications that had cared for the people's health for generations.

When the river was in flood, the village became an island, the villagers going from forested knoll to knoll with their dugout canoes; fishing, collecting fire wood, and trapping game. As the floods receded, the times of plenty began. Quantities of fish were congregated in the remaining pools left by the departing waters where they could be easily scooped and netted, filling every family's larder. The ooze that covered the margins was turned into the heavy soil to produce just the right mixture for bumper tuber crops. The forests opened, the small knolls becoming forested expanses where firewood, food, and medicinal plants, as well as monkeys and antelope were more accessible.

As the river returned to its banks, the snakes left the village, where they had concentrated during the floods, following the rodents that fled the advancing waters and looked to the villagers' silos as the best refuge from the wet season. As the river abated, life seemed to follow the snakes out of the village, expanding like a head-pan of soaking cassava. The paths and roads were now freed of their watery covering. Businesses could accelerate to a new level, no longer limited to that merchandise that could be carried in a canoe. Markets and bars were now well supplied. Bush taxi transport re-emerged. People were able to travel outside, and outsiders able to visit. The villagers organized all variety of celebrations from weddings to male or female circumcision ceremonies.

But for all the accelerated activity that followed the retreating waters, like scavengers following a retreating army, life had no sparkle. There was little to excite the dullest youth and Simon was far from being sluggish; neither in body nor in mind.

During his Father's youth there were vast rubber plantations above the flood line that provided employment and even the opportunity for advancement along with a modest level of wealth. These were intermingled with oil palm plantations that were rumored to be the wave of the future. But then another oil came and superseded all else: "petrol".

When abundant near-shore petroleum was discovered, Government lost all interest in everything else. Petrol, petrol, petrol . . . Truly the Big Men felt the gods had smiled when they brought them petrol. As they said: *chop na chop* and those who could, be they big or small, chopped their part of the "national pie". Petrol dominated all. There was no more farming, no more small business, no more textiles or groundnuts; there was petrol.

As the country took its myopic look at development, the cities swelled like the river in flood while the villages shriveled, many atrophying to nothingness. The mega-cites spawned by petrol were countries unto themselves and the sole place, or so it seemed, where a young man could find life that sparkled.

So it was, after his eighteenth flood, Simon followed the ebbing waters out of the village, out of the district, and out of the province. Along with hundreds of thousands of other young men similar to himself, he headed to the mega-cities on an almost holy mission—unerringly, like flies drawn to offal. Simon followed the well-worn path to the land of colorful lights, modern music, beautiful women, and, of course, wealth.

His first introduction to El Dorado was an unbelievable traffic jam that started more than twenty kilometers outside the city limits. Simon sucked in the hot muggy, pollution-ridden air along with the score of other profusely sweating passengers in the minibus, as it painstakingly inched toward their destination. This sluggish progress was completely halted on four occasions as they stopped at police checkpoints when, somehow thankfully, all the passengers had to disembark and present their papers and luggage to uniformed officers looking for any tiny reason to extort a few cents from the fatigued travelers.

Simon managed to avoid any bribes and finally alighted in one of the many taxi parks with absolutely no idea what to do next. His first reaction was to enquire about where to find people from his village, as different tribal and ethnic groups tended to congregate in common areas of big cities. However, when he asked the roving vendors, shop keepers, barmen, and restauranteurs that frequented the taxi park; the best he could get was guttural intonation that said more through mannerisms than words, "If you have no money, go away".

Almost like a homing pigeon on a wind-blown night, Simon zig-zagged the trash-strewn muddy streets of the city, at times nearly gagging from the rich aroma emanating from the open gutters filled with plastic bags, disposable nappies, and who knows what. He followed not his nose nor his eyes but his ears, keeping them pitched to the unique sing-song rhythms of his native tongue. At last, seemingly after hours of mindless wandering, he heard a cadence from his village. Like a bat homing-in, he identified two young girls selling cigarettes from enameled platters perched delicately on their heads. Feigning the need for a stick of cigarettes, he approached the girls and greeted them in his, and he hoped, their native tongue. It worked. The reaction was nearly immediate and the girls' stoic faces thawed into great smiles as they knew they were with one of their own.

Simon introduced himself and explained with great brevity his pilgrimage to the big city to find his better life. Although the girls giggled as though they had heard the story many times before, they were most polite and respectful as though they were still in the village. They told Simon most of the émigrés from the East were in the southern suburbs, a euphemism for slums. They gave him, most importantly, the name and street number of the man who served as the local chief of their tribe; apparently a wise man named Isaiah.

It took nearly half of his cash reserves and three different rust-bucket yellow city taxis to reach the southern suburbs. For each taxi, he would share the small car with four or five other passengers and get off at the closest point to his destination given the combined routes required by all the passengers—a technique called *ramassage,* which meant you did not pay full fare and did not, of course, get all the way to your destination at one go. Each change of taxis was like a step into a different world. The first vehicle was somehow in more-or-less workable condition and it dropped him at a junction of two busy and well-lit streets. Here the only taxis going his way were real heaps with windows that did not roll up and doors that did not close properly. This time he was dropped off at the intersection of two pot-holed streets made of a mixture of asphalt, stone, and laterite; surrounded by dilapidated buildings and ramshackle shops; but nevertheless, the streets and sidewalks a bustle with people of all shapes and descriptions. Here he had to wait nearly an hour for a vehicle that honestly made one wonder how it managed to make its way down any street, not to mention the rough and rock-strewn path he was now instructed to follow. The vehicle had a body that looked like it had come through a war, a sprung frame, no windows except a badly cracked windshield. The seats were some springs covered with cardboard and there were seven people crammed into the car at various angles and with great contortions. When he wiggled out of the back and paid the driver, he found himself in a dark and damp area that reminded him of the village at flood season. The ground was soft under foot, but the scent was that of rot and defecation as opposed to the clean earthy aroma of the flood. And, this was just the outskirts of the suburb.

From here he had to go on by "*moto-taxi*"—well-worn 100 cc motorcycles that skillfully maneuvered the narrow lanes and even narrower stick bridges that crisscrossed the fetid sewers, drains, and canals. When he finally dismounted the *moto*, he found himself in a seemingly deserted path with shanties on both sides, nothing one would think of as homes that actually had a street number. But, as he was to clearly see in the morning, when the Government had undertaken the recent census, they had painted large white numbers on each and every structure to avoid double counts. These census reference numbers had become the new house numbers.

Simon was pleasantly surprised when, after knocking repeatedly at the door of his destination, fearing the energy of his hailing might make the door fall aside, the entry cracked open revealing a welcoming yellow light from a kerosene lamp and an even more welcoming smile as he greeted the lady behind the door in his native tongue.

He was indeed welcomed in true country fashion by Isaiah and his wife. They had obviously been sipping tea and listening to the radio in the small and brimming space that served as a combination living and sleeping room; the cooing of children behind the wall indicating that the most modest abode had at least one other room where an unknown number of young-ones dozed.

Strangely, although a complete stranger, he was readily shepherded into the home with no misgivings or trepidation. It was ironic that simply speaking the same language, being an attestation to common ethnicity, was sufficient to open doors to strangers far from home, whereas this would not have been the case in the village where all spoke the same language.

Isaiah was a shoemaker. He had a kiosk some few hundred meters away along a more commercial pathway. While his profession apparently provided enough to put food on the table and some sort of roof over their heads, it was not his profession that had led to him be the leader of his tribe. His grandfather had been a *Tchinda*, a *serviteur* or steward, to the old, now deceased Chief; the current Chief's father. This somewhat feeble link was sufficient for him to have the traditional roots to be a city leader for his people.

As Simon looked upon the elder man in the golden and flickering lamp light, it was clear that he indeed merited the respect that he must have to be able to be the tribe's focal point in this rather large city. He had a kind and knowledgeable face with an appearance that made one feel immediately as though he personally cared about whatever topic was being discussed. Simon hoped this was the face of honestly and not the face of a politician.

When Simon recounted his tale, he realized the face was indeed the face of sincerity. Isaiah was truly interested in helping minimize the potential stress and pitfalls so often encountered when villagers came to the city looking for the pot of gold at the end of the rainbow—more often than not finding the pot, if they found it at all, empty and full of holes. Simon sensed Isaiah remembered the hopes of youth and the desire to look over the next hill and behind the closed door.

After Simon finished graphically displaying his eagerness to find a new life and the path to riches, Isaiah, under the knowing gaze of his wife, kindly took effort not to be too discouraging, yet to paint a realistic picture of the difficulties in finding even substandard accommodation in the city; not to mention work. He apologized from the onset for not being able to offer Simon a room himself. As was nearly always the case, as a city-dweller, those still in the village thought of him as rich; albeit this was far, far from the truth. As a city-dweller, all thought of him as living in luxury and with access to all the better things in life; this, as well, far from the truth. But the truth had little to do with the process and, with these images clear in their minds, his family and friends from the village, completely unannounced, sent their children and younger siblings to him for him to give them the good life. For him to feed and house. For him to put into school. For him to clothe. As it turned out, although he and his wife only had two children of their own, there were a total of seven children in the hovel. And, it was only the absolute physical impossibility of taking-in another child that had stemmed the flow; the economic possibilities of supporting such a flock never entering into the equation.

So it was that Isaiah sent Simon, although it was now late at night, to the house, such as it was, of Alfred. Isaiah told Simon that Alfred worked as a casual laborer, loading or unloading lorries in the industrial area. He lived not far away in a similar hovel that he shared with four or five other laborers. However, as one of this group had recently been killed in a traffic accident, there should be a space for Simon to lay his head.

Simon received nearly as warm a greeting at Alfred's as he had at Isaiah's. He was beginning to think that this city life was even friendlier than the much-flaunted life in the village. Alfred's shanty was constructed of *carabot*; rough-hewn planks for the walls. The roof was poor quality metal sheets and the floor was pounded earth. There were two small rooms with the partition separating them made of a combination of cardboard and tin sheets hammered from cans. There was a rickety table with four chairs in one corner. This was made of unfinished wood that had once been white but was now oily black due to soot, dust, and palm oil. In another corner there was a kerosene cooker and stone mortar and pestle that served as the cooking area. The remainder of the room was occupied by two small wooden beds with collapsed and dirty foam mattresses—the beds serving both for sleeping and as settees when the room was used more for eating and communing than slumber. The back room had a series of boxes and well-worn suitcases against the wall and three mattresses adorning the floor.

With the endorsement of Isaiah, Simon was offered one of these to pass his first night in the city.

The night was short and before sunrise the neighborhood began to stir. Roosters crowed, children giggled, dogs barked, goats bleated, pots rattled, people hacked and coughed; the air filled with a haze of charcoal smoke laced with kerosene and motorcycle fumes. As the grilling sun peaked over the lip of the world, this harsh chemical perfume was nearly replaced by an almost sweet bouquet of sewage and other sludge that began to percolate in the open gutters that seemingly ran everywhere.

This was an ambiance far removed from the earthly smell of the village and river to which Simon was accustomed; the village sunrise welcomed by the chants of the fisherman as they came to the landings with their evening's catch. He tried to stretch the aches from his body, these coming as much from his arduous journey as the lumpy mattress on the dirt floor. As his eyes blinked away the night's grit and were able to take in his surroundings, he was moderately surprised to notice the recumbent forms on the two neighboring mattresses. One, rolled in a colorful, if soiled sheet, was that of a content and snoring man of his age, apparently one of his new roommates. The other jumble was less readily defined, but appeared to be two intertwined forms under a grey matted blanket. He would soon learn that this was another roommate with his girlfriend of the moment.

He moved his focus further to his surroundings and found these to be shabby, or worse. Feeling the need to heed nature's call after oily street food in taxi parks yesterday, he half stumbled into the main room and found Albert sitting on his bed, smoking the stub of a cigarette. His new mate directed him to the back where there was a pit latrine shared by the adjoining households. He entered the palm frond enclosure with care, knowing that many feel "close is good enough", when it comes to using the pit. Here this would have seemed to be good advice as the rotting wood that supported the user over the hole was questionable at best. Moreover, the pit was so full that it looked as though the maggots might actually jump onto your drawers. Nevertheless, apparently every one respected the community and used the hole, so he hesitantly stepped on the wood as he lowered his trousers.

Successfully avoiding the much feared dunking in the latrine, he returned to the room to see what now lay in store. There was not much of a morning routine; the mates, male and female, just seemed to evaporate into the growing morning heat. Just before midday he accompanied Albert to the lorry park to see about any small jobs loading or unloading trucks, feeling the odds were a bit better than normal since this was cacao season. Simon still did not really know with whom he was living; knowing the names of no one except Albert, and knowing pitifully little about him.

Nevertheless, Isaiah's words appeared to hold some weight and Albert, though guarded, was willing enough to discuss life in the city with Simon. If just a glance around the surroundings were not sufficient, Albert vividly and articulately described the immense difficulties in surviving. Everyone was chasing the same get-rich-quick rainbow; most with equally dismal results. The simple fact of the matter was that there were thousands of applicants for every opportunity and while you waited for your time to come, you were victimized by thieves, rapists, and swindlers; not to mention the fraternity of businessmen who extorted unbelievably high rents for unbelievably squalid conditions.

The opportunities were indeed quite limited, but there was just enough to keep people dangling in the web of hope. The informal market was full to overflowing and no one could penetrate it, not only due to its over-capacity, but also to the fact that is was controlled by Market Queens who held monopolies on all products and produce that flowed through these channels. There were occasional openings in the multitude of bars, restaurants, chophouses, and cabarets that dotted the urban and suburban areas. But these were only arranged from the inside; the new employee obliged to give up at least a quarter of the minuscule salary to the insider who "fixed" the job. The real object of all the émigrés' attention were the jobs servicing the ballooning petroleum industry. There were literally thousands of itinerant laborers pumping mud, shoveling sand, pounding nails, and mixing concrete to support the distended and bloated industry and its core of elite technicians and capitalists from here and abroad.

Each day well before sunrise there were scores, if not hundreds, of young men who congregated outside the iron gates and aluminum roofing sheet fences that surrounded the compounds of these sometimes fly-by-night establishments that paid for an hour's work more than most made in a week. Many days the iron gates never opened and the men drifted away as the thermometer mounted and with their despair. On those days when there was hiring, the gates opened to reveal troops of bludgeon-armed security guards who herded the men like cattle into a strictly enforced queue. Strictly enforced, unless you slipped one of the guards a few bills and then made your way to the head of the line at your own risk.

Nevertheless, as Albert put it so well, "That's the only game in town". Waiting, fighting, bribing, and pandering to try to get ahead. In an end-justifies-the-means society there were opportunities for wealth. But at what cost? Ninety-eight percent of the would-be *nouveau-riche* ended up either dead, broken, or disenfranchised. There were really few if any occupational safety standards and regulations; many laborers moving about heavy construction sites with nothing more than flip-flops and baggy shorts. The cases of work-related injuries and even deaths were numerous. However, these were less numerous than the deaths resulting from muggings, drug overdoses, malaria, and other seemingly routine health problems that could not be adequately cared for in the teeming ghettos. And those who managed to survive with their lives were psychologically changed to the point where they often disenfranchised themselves from their past, if their past did not shut the door first. But these were the fortunes of the game and Simon was in town to play and to win.

It was thus, according to "the game", that Simon saw the days merge into weeks, and the weeks into months as he became more and more immersed in "the game". Indeed, immersed was the word. Like being immersed in the river, the objective was to keep your head above water. This was not a baptismal dousing when you bobbed up and down a few times as the priest held your hand in the shallows and blessed your soul, this was real immersion and there were strong currents that could easily suck you under.

The way to survive was to establish a routine and to keep busy. In this environment, Simon found survival itself nearly a full-time job. He was able to adopt the mattress at Albert's as his own by making weekly contributions to the costs of living; rent, food, and water, the latter carried by children using jerry cans, toting the essential liquid from a pay-for-use tap almost two kilometers from the hovel. He was able to meet his financial obligations by task work washing lorries at the Total Gas Station near the closest taxi park.

Although a congenial member of the rather bizarre household, he shunned the temptations to assuage his frustrations, trying hard to economize his few coins. He would politely decline the offer to visit the local *Arkie* den where this burning near pure-alcohol beverage was sold at bargain prices. He would kindly pass on the "doobie" of mind-blowing *Bhanga* (marijuana), which his roommates were able to score at family prices at the Lepers' market. He would gently decline the offers from the teenage hookers who also came to the city to find the pot of gold and only found the offal of the ghetto.

He would rather rise well before the sun and rinse of the night's sweat with a bucket of nearly clean water before having a cup of tea and crust of stale bread, then walk nearly eight kilometers to the industrial area. Taking taxis, even *moto* taxies, would be prohibitively expensive and walking was the only option. He would then join the queues at any of the many service enterprises; almost like the lottery, selecting the gate outside which to wait in the hopes, nearly always in vain, that Lady Luck would smile on that day and a real job would be found. By mid-day the chances were too slim and the temperature too hot to continue the wait for naught.

Simon would start his trek home, breaking it at the Total Station where he would work for at least four hours scrubbing mud-incrusted lorries and taxis for a pittance. He would stumble back to his mattress by eight or nine with a grand profit of one to two hundred francs (approximately 50 cents US).

This was the routine that dogged Simon's life for weeks and months. There was always that small ember of hope glowing in his gut that made him get up after only a few hours of sleep and force his feet, one in front of the other, as he dragged himself through the day and back to a grungy mattress in a grungy neighborhood in the night. The realities of the city were not able to douse this ember. It may dim, but it still provided enough warmth to keep Simon going.

Then the ember's tepid glow was replaced by the burning heat of fever as he finally succumbed to the disease that thrived in the water-ridden byways that accounted for the sodden ghetto. Mosquitoes were simply a fact of life. Like the flies, they were everywhere. Every morning every one awoke scratching the lumps that remained from the evening's feedings. For most it was only a matter of time before an attack came. The disease could come and go quickly or it could deliver a devastating punch that left most of its victims comatose and near death.

Simon seemed to have been luckier than most and survived months without even the slightest symptoms. But then it came with a vengeance. In just a few hours he was transformed from a strong, if fatigued seeker-of -jobs and part-time truck washer into a shaking mass of jelly, lying in a pool of sweat. He had no grain of strength left; not even enough awareness to know where he was or what was happening. He was on the verge.

Fortunately, Albert and the current group of roommates had enough humanity to do something; and there were not too many options. When they found him in fetal position in the morning, they sent for a child with a *pousse-pousse*—a handcart with bicycle tires—and dumped his body into the cart, thereafter helping the young operator push its charge to the nearest clinic more than an hour of hard work away.

When the clinic staff did not want to admit Simon because he did not have his papers or any money, his roommates simply dumped him on the steps and went home. Thereupon, the clinic could not, as Albert knew, leave him. The nurses indeed finally half towed, half carried him to a crowded ward where they forced some aspirin and *nivaquine* down his throat.

This would have been the end, and truly end of Simon, if this act had played itself out. But Lady Luck, who had not smiled in the employment line, did smile in the clinic. Simon happened to be stuck in the ward just before the daily visit by one of the public health doctors from the nearby hospital. She saw the life-and-death battle that was going on inside Simon's body and quickly gave orders for him to be immediately transferred to the emergency room at the hospital. Here, in only a slightly less crowded and befouled room, he was put on an IV and kept under close observation.

Nearly a day later, although Simon had no notion of time, he awoke coughing as though choking, having slight memories of dreams of being strangled by a giant brown boa. His fever broke and he was slowly able to take solid food and regain a bit of his strength.

As he recuperated in the cramped and chaotic hospital, being moved from the emergency ward to a general ward which was even more bedraggled, he felt as though he were seeing the world through a dirty veil. Everything seemed to be the color of dirt. The walls, regardless their original color, were now dirt-brown after the caresses of thousands of the unwashed. The bedding, probably once white, was now clay colored after far too many washings in water filled with sediment. The floor was covered with bits and pieces of mud carried by the constant flow of the sick and their families.

Surprisingly this veil did not depress Simon but rather gave him a new ember simmering in his belly. This was the color of the great river, the color of home. He had seen the city. He had confronted the city. It was time to go home. The game was over: "Match nil".

Regal Responsibilities

HE WAS WORRIED. THINGS might not work out so well after all. He had thought he had covered all the bases and done the right thing. Now he wasn't sure. There was no question that the decision had been the best one and the best for his people, but what would be the ultimate consequences?

Tü-Fâm was, relatively speaking, a thriving area comprised of over 25 villages and he was the King with strong support from both the people and the *Notables*. This was key as, though it may not have been common knowledge, it was really the *Notables,* the traditional pedigreed gentry, who held the reins of power.

Tradition was a funny thing. In Colonialists' culture it would have been the eldest son to "chop the chair" and inherit his sire's place (primogeniture-ship). Here there was no dauphin. According to custom, the King could choose from among any of his male children. Under the colonial system, he, as not the first-born, would have been free of any regal obligations. However, this was Tü-Fâm and his Father had named him as his successor from among his many sons, several older than he. This nomination needed to be, and was endorsed by the *Notables* as they were the ones who took on the young Chief's training once his Father had passed and he had assumed the path to the throne.

This path was neither particularly quick nor easy. The Chief, or King-to-be, had to go through an exhausting indoctrination, a mix of initiation and tutelage. During this process, the incoming regent was taught all the secrets and secret customs of the tribe. At the same time, he was offered a long parade of the Kingdom's most winsome maidens; those who became pregnant becoming wives.

Indeed, the wives, they were many. Not only did you inherit your Father's wives, and, as in his case, come to the table with your own wife, you immediately gained a covey of nubile maids nearly overnight. But this was a digression, the *Notables* were the complication and truly worrisome. Governing a community where there was a figurehead with real and presumed power in the foreground, and a more powerful group in the background, often completely hidden from view and knowledge, was not the ideal arrangement, when one was trying to keep "what was best for the most" at the forefront.

The *Notables*, or the Nine Wise Men as they were sometimes called, were a shadowy group composed of successors from within the tribe's most important families. They not only introduced a new Chief to his responsibilities, but they also served as an absolute judge and jury that oversaw how the Chief executed these responsibilities. Often, for serious matters, they were consulted beforehand to avoid any misunderstanding that, after the fact, could have dire consequences. Rarely if ever would a Chief knowingly and publicly go against the wishes of the *Notables*.

Not only did the *Notables* directly control significant wealth and power in the villages, but they were also the traditional keepers of the order, the inner circle that had the power and wherewithal to remove a Chief. And a Chief, being a King for life, could only be removed through death.

The Chief had his *Tchinda*, his principal advisor and assistant. But while the *Tchinda* was an essential individual in administering the affairs of the community, he held no real traditional power and could advise the Chief, but not influence to any great degree the *Notables*.

Now, there was a very serious matter at hand. The Chief and his *Tchinda* were clearly of one mind on this issue and both knew that there was but one responsible course to follow. But the position of the *Notables* on the matter remained an enigma.

The issue was in fact quite complex.

Like many parts of the well-endowed country, Tü-Fâm was blessed with considerable natural resources. While smallholder farming was the primary economic activity for the majority of the community, there were known reserves of still-to-be-exploited minerals. Global mineral markets were booming and the politicians and deciders in the country's capital were in a hurry to tap into major profits before the markets dipped. International investors were well known for their magnanimity to the causes and accounts of the country's leadership. These same investors were most insistent the country should shake off the shackles of the past and become an emerging economy in the world market, starting of course by immediately extracting all possible minerals and shipping these off-shore for processing via their conglomerates.

In the prevailing economic environment, digging up these stones today would reap great wealth for those at the top, with considerable overflow sloshing downhill to the Chief and his inner circle.

He could almost feel the glove-soft kid leather seats of a brand new, shiny black Mercedes that would be such a welcome change from his old Peugeot. He could build many houses in the provincial capital and lease these out to government projects at inflated prices, establishing a cash flow stream that would serve his ever-so-many children for years to come. He could send his oldest kids to school in France and his first wife on an extended vacation to Geneva. He could do almost whatever he wanted and the *Notables* would be able to keep pace with him franc for franc; the heads of Tü-Fâm could become unbelievably rich and do absolutely nothing but stand on the sidelines and watch the bulldozers scrape away the soil.

What's more, the Company would build a new health center, three primary schools strategically located in different villages, as well as a secondary school not far from the Palace. All would share in the wealth. It was a win-win situation. And, all thoughts and discussion should have stopped there.

However, the Chief's youngest wife, the daughter of a neighboring Chief, had planted a poisoned seed. She was well educated and had initially resisted marrying the much older Chief, wanting to pursue her studies and go on to law school. But her Father had applied all possible pressure on her, as his most attractive and highly prized daughter, to make her marry his old neighbor. This union would assure amiable arrangements between the adjoining communities and guarantee his own people access to needed water from the small river that separated their two kingdoms.

This marriage of convenience had turned into much more over the two years since she had become the Chief's junior wife. He understood all too well her opposition to entering into the life at the Palace.

He, too, had been a student preparing for university when he had been called to assume his Father's throne. He had seriously considered fleeing, but his Father's old *Tchinda,* now long since passed himself to join his much-loved ruler, had played most adroitly the guilt card, convincing the young and impressionable student that he had been born to be King and to do anything else with his life would be to insult God who had put him on this Earth to serve. In spite of himself, he had acquiesced and was now the one seated on the teak and ebony carved stool. But not a day went by when he did not ask himself if he had made the right decision. He knew he had paid a high price.

He had been among the few students preparing for university who was already married. Tradition demanded that a man have a house, at least five head of cattle, and funds for a bride price before he could ask a woman, or more correctly her father, for her hand in marriage. These prerequisites put marriage out of reach for most young men until such a time as they had gainful employment and had amassed some savings; in most cases, until several years after they finished their education. The Chief had been lucky and was able to side-step these hard-to-achieve requirements. As a King's son, a prince in other cultures, he was assured an adequate level of wealth to be able to provide the dowry for a wife whenever he wished. And he had wished to do so while still in school. He had loved Jeanne for as long as he could remember. They had grown up together, her father an off-license owner and coffee trader living close to the Palace. They were like Jack and Jill, almost joined at the hip. They had gathered wild fruit in the King's private forest, stuffed themselves on avocados and mangos during the height of the season, swam in the river while their mothers washed clothes nearby, and roamed in the savannah hunting wild mushrooms.

Given her innate special abilities and her families' prominence, she, among all girls her age, had advanced in her studies and kept pace, step by step with the Chief-to-be. It seemed like the most natural thing in the world for them to marry, and they did.

Whether one of the frivolities of youth or the ability of youth to avoid reality, for whatever reason, they had not thought about the Chiefdom-ship nor the Palace as they planned to wed; their thoughts fully occupied by dreams of diplomas and children. When he had acceded to return to assume the throne, he had thoroughly discussed this transition with her.

She was a child of the community. She knew the traditions and knew the lifestyles. She knew what to expect and, for all intents and purposes, she entered into the situation with her eyes wide open, encouraging her young husband to assume the robes of the Chief.

Sadly, things are seldom as they seem. It was hard enough sharing her life with scores of other females, but it was even more difficult to be cooped up in the Palace for weeks and months on end, almost never having a chance to get away. When she did, it was only to the boring provincial capital and not the nation's political capital in the beautiful central mountains nor its economic capital on the bustling coast. Life as the First Wife turned out to be insufferable.

This misery completely changed the once open and happy mushroom-hunting girl into a bitter and jealous middle aged lady with a spirit much older and meaner than the age of her now unkempt body. The Chief's throne served as a bigger and bigger wedge between the Chief and the First Wife, the former occupying more and more of his time with the affairs of State and the latter succumbing to the common pastimes of the Palace of rumor-mongering and back-stabbing.

Then, when the Chief's Junior Wife entered the Palace, the dynamics changed completely. Here was a young and vivacious woman who was an intellectual equal with the First Wife and even more of a political reactionary. She had a quick mind and an even quicker tongue, always ready to comment on any topic; a trait the

Chief found especially intriguing in a setting where women still knelt to the King and spoke only when spoken to, and only then through a covered mouth.

Francine, the Junior Wife, was a breath of fresh air. She was also a harbinger of another world. She brought with her a profound commitment to social and environmental responsibility—quite a different mix from the traditional responsibilities into which the Chief had been indoctrinated.

On quiet evenings, as all in the Palace and out settled down to sleep, she would sit on the veranda with the Chief and explain why and how people should take care of Mother Earth. She spoke of pollution, deforestation, desertification, urbanization, too little water and too many people, and too many chiefs and not enough Indians. Things that had been black and white assumed shades of gray. Absolute truths now came into doubt. What was once the only way to do things suddenly became one of many ways to do things. His view of the universe had changed.

Then the stone seekers came on the scene and his life was turned upside down. In another time it would have been automatic. The outside investors would have prepared their arrangements, agreements, and contracts. These would come to the Chief pre-approved by the highest leadership. The Chief and *Notables* would keep up appearances, call a community meeting, discuss the way forward, and then unanimously approve all the arrangements as the money was transferred to their accounts.

And then Francine raised her voice. What of the people displaced by the excavations? What of the erosion spoiling the river and streams? What of the loss of trees as the land is cleared? When the stones are gone, how will the land be left? When the stones are gone, what will the people do?

This wasn't fair. These were not questions that were supposed to be asked. It wasn't supposed to be complicated, it was easy; as easy as digging a hole.

But Francine had planted the seed and it grew in the Chief's mind. What were the answers? What was the best course of action? What should he do?

He talked in confidence with his trusted *Tchinda*. What he lacked in formal education, his *Tchinda* more than made up for in empathy and common sense. And, when you took a real long honest view of the situation it really wasn't so complicated, the stones were best left where they were, where they had been for the past twenty-five generations and where they should be for the next twenty-five. His choice was clear.

But what of the *Notables*? His new-found scruples would cost the Group of Nine millions of francs. They would not take this loss lightly. In fact they would not accept it at all. This would be the feared rift between spokesperson and the people for whom he is perceived to speak. This would be a chasm opening between the Chief and the *Notables*, a chasm above which the Chief was teetering and into which he worried he would fall.

His *Tchinda* warned him sternly to avoid meeting privately with the *Notables* and to be careful of what he ate or drank as the *Notables* most often removed a troublesome Chief with poison. He could trust no one. He must become a recluse in his chambers until the *Tchinda* could talk some sense into the *Notables* and they could see how the Chief's decision not to go ahead with digging up the stones would ultimately be best for the whole community including the *Notables*, their families, and their children's children.

The Chief heeded the warning and cloistered himself in his private chambers only seeing the trusted duo of his *Tchinda* and Francine. He spent his time pacing and thinking. Worried and fearful to go out, even afraid to receive Jeanne when she called upon him for fear she would leave some powerful *juju* fetish, or similar evil charm, in his rooms or some toxic wizard's powders in his pantry. Things were not good.

The walls moved in on him; the crowing of the cock supervising the chickens scratching aimlessly outside his windows sounded like an evil omen; he needed to do something, he must do something; but what? The *Notables* were certainly not doing nothing. There was money at stake and lots of money. The *Notables* were on the scent of these riches like a Palace dog ferreting out a cane rat; and like a good hunting dog, they would grip their prey by the nape of its neck and not let go. They were not doing nothing and he was. Things were not good.

With a sense of gratification, his ill ease and worries were at least temporarily put aside as Francine brought in a plate of her special and most appreciated *taro*, cooked and mashed coco yams. This pasty dish was served with a deceptively complicated yellow sauce that contained over a score of unique herbs and spices that made it a much-needed elixir for the worried Chief.

He ran his fingers around the outside of the volcano-shaped heap of *taro*, until he had a healthy grayish ball. He then delicately dipped this into the volcano's crater which was brimming with yellow gravy. The dripping ball then quickly plopped into an eagerly awaiting mouth. Hungrily the Chief ate ball after ball until the plate was spotless and he was most contentedly satiated.

His head felt light and his toes tingled a bit as he kicked off his slippers and stretched out on his raffia bamboo day bed. The cock crowed one last time as his tongue swelled and the curtain fell on his world. In the distance there was the purring of a powerful motor as Francine turned the key of her new shiny black Mercedes.

A Farmer's Song

THOSE WHO SAY THE rooster crows to herald the dawn obviously have been up just once at dawn and happened to have heard a cock crow. This was like the folks who said that white people are smarter than blacks, or everything European is better than things that are African; gross generalizations at best, down-right prejudicial at worst, but this really doesn't apply to the old rooster. Yet the old roster can be just as irritating. When you hear his call, at all hours of the night and early morning, if it resonates from across the village, it may be a rather pleasant reminder that all is well with the Earth. When the scraggly old bird is right outside your window, its oscillating decibels can be like a dull knife cutting through tough fabric, the fabric being your ear drums.

Nevertheless, the song of the rooster was part of the morning anthem that accompanied the routine of starting a new day. The village would begin awakening well before the sun crept over the eastern hills and then magically vaulted into the sky. Dogs would come from their crannies, stretch and sniff the air, and then stiffly amble off looking for scraps. Sheep and goats began to appear like termites after a rain. As their owners opened the small pens where they had passed the night, they would troop off looking for anything to chew. The smell of smoke would rise as hearths were lit. Shutters would be opened to air out the mud-block houses as children took straw mattresses outside to dry in the sun after a somewhat sodden night when the one or more of the several children sharing the mattress would "have an accident". Old folks would move their raffia stools into the best spots to warm themselves in the early sun while the hardiest would pick up hoe or machete and head to the field to do some work before breakfast.

The rooster was only a small part of the orchestra that so skillfully played the song of the farmer. There was a myriad of other birds that chirped, chattered, and called to join the cacophony. There were the happy cries of children playing that infused the ringing of the old gong at the school and the bell at the church, all joining forces to make the music that had become synonymous with life for the farmer.

It was nearly always the same. The cadence would change with the seasons, slowing with the rains when the mornings were dull and wet, but never coming to a standstill. The actors and scenes would change, but the heart remained true. The village was a village of farmers, each and every member in one way or another beholding to the crops and the mysteries of nature. For generations the villagers had tended coffee plantations, plantain and banana stands, maize and groundnut fields, along with cassava, yams, taro, sweet potatoes, and a whole gamut of vegetables. There were also the palm trees for oil and palm wine as well as the raffia forests for wine, fibers, and thatch. In short, it all was there. But for how long? This was the question that occupied Jerome's thoughts as he watched his wife reheat the evening meal to serve the family this cool and sun-lit morning, as he watched his eldest daughter sweep the compound with a bamboo broom, as he watched his younger daughters head off to the stream with big head-pans to fetch water for the up-coming day, as he watched his sons getting ready to go to the fields after a filling meal of maize meal and vegetables, as he too prepared to go to his farms and do as he had done yesterday and the day before and as his Father had done. This was a day like so many others, but also a day unlike any others.

This afternoon the Chief had called all the people to come to the Palace to discuss with the representative of the Provincial Governor what amounted to the village's future. This was the day when the village would hear the Chief's decision. This was the day when Jerome would look into his future and know if he would be able to continue to follow his Father's footsteps. Today was one of those days like when there was a new paramount chief or a new sultan, when life could change and, as he knew all too well, change did not automatically mean change for the better.

Farmers were used to being pawns in larger games, played by those in power. They were at the bottom of the pecking-order, subject to the ploys and whims of all above, and those above were many. There were sub-chiefs, notables, chiefs, district officers, provincial officers, and then a whole colony of those at higher levels of whom Jerome had only heard, but had never seen.

The ecology of farmers was simple. They were the herbivores, the prey of the carnivores. They were the bottom of the food chain, but they were also the core of the food chain. What would the predatory politicians and their boot-licking *Tchindas* eat if there were no farmers to feed them? But, of course, they never thought about this. Their only thoughts were for themselves. How could they make more money, have more wives, and enjoy more power? And, alas, today Jerome's village had become the object of these princes of profit.

And now today, after returning from a trip to the capital where he had encountered the decision-makers, power-brokers, and money-givers, the Chief was to tell the village what their future would be; what was to be the destiny of the farms and the farmers.

This matter of such great importance had such a seemingly innocent beginning. Some Chinese agronomists had visited the village over a year ago to provide training for farmers, teaching new integrated farming practices that could, in the opinion of experts, lead to significantly greater yields. No one realized the Chinese had also been charged with gathering information from all the villages they visited, assessing each as a possible site for large Chinese agribusinesses. The news filtered back that Jerome's village was among the top three choices.

Initially, this top ranking had filled all with great joy, like collectively winning the lottery. After all, a big multi-national firm investing millions in their village could not but help each and every member of the village in one way or another. There would be money, money, money. Paved roads, a real school, a health center, and piped water—all the amenities they had grown to expect from the new modern politicians, but things that had yet to materialize. Surely this outside venture capital would be the answer to their prayers and the cure for their suffering; although suffering might be too strong a word to describe the otherwise quite idyllic life of the village.

However, and most worrisome, as more and more news dribbled down the village network, it seemed as though there were real questions about how these people would actually undertake their investment should they choose Jerome's village. It seemed that over on the eastern side of the country there had been a similar investigation for Chinese investors in the mining sector. But, when the approvals were given and the contracts signed, nothing, absolutely nothing, seeped down to the village. Quite to the contrary, the village *per se* ceased to exist; replaced by a camp for Chinese workers who came to work in the mine. No local people were involved in any way what-so-ever. The bosses, supervisors, drivers, laborers, cooks, and bottle washers were all Chinese. No one from the village found a job and the village itself was forced to relocate to make room for the labor camp. Could this happen to Jerome's village?

Today was the telling moment as nearly all the village assembled at the Palace to hear the Chief. The congregation waited in a semicircle in the shade of prune trees until the exalted Chief would receive them. After a suitable period of deferral, the Chief appeared, flanked by his *Tchindas*, with a representative of the provincial government hanging in the shadows to oversee the transactions.

When the Chief started by extolling the ancestors and recounting the village's history of the past five generations, all knew that no good news would be forthcoming. True to expectations, after over half an hour of monotonous droning about the blessing of the forefathers and the central government, the village's Head announced, with great humility, that the village had been selected by the Chinese for the site of a big new farm.

To the Northeast of the village there was a large wetland plain in the shadow of the Mount Bapit. Cattle grazed on the plain while the villagers had their farms around its margins and up the first part of the slopes of the mountain. This entire area was now the object of a project to develop a big rice farm.

Although the country had many suitable areas for rice, and consumption of rice was rapidly growing, the country had a major deficit in rice supply which was made up for by importing large quantities of rice from Southeast Asia and North America. To improve the country's balance of payments and solidify commercial links with China, efforts were underway to increase national rice production by tenfold.

Albeit rice was rarely eaten in the maize-consuming area where Jerome lived, and farmers had no experience raising watery crops like rice, government had decided to build the massive pilot rice farm here. Not only would this take over all the grazing and farm land in the plain and surrounding areas, but the farm would be fully operated by the Chinese. Their worst fears had come to pass, they would lose their land and livelihoods at one fell swoop.

The Chief couched all this in the terms of economic development for the village, reminding all they would receive an indemnity of five hundred dollars; truly, as the Chief knew well, a huge amount of cash for one family to receive at one time. Alas, he had no answer to the questions of his people as to what they would do with no farms. Everyone understood that this was the end of the village as they had known it, regardless of all the ancestors' blessings the Chief had used for embellishing his decision.

In fact, within a few days, under the pretext of needing medical treatment, the Chief vanished, reportedly traveling to France on an extended absence. In his place, the restructuring of the village was taken over by a sub-chief who seemed to have a Chinese twin in the person of one of the principal investors who had come to ensure that the needed changes would be promptly made so the Chinese could begin building dams and dikes in the plain.

Jerome and his family were thrown into a sea of uncertainty, not knowing where or how to go. He and all the villagers were at a complete loss. What could be done? What were the options? Many found no answers other than using the windfall from the government to buy volumes of beer and schnapps to assuage their woes.

Jerome was among the lucky. He already had a second business selling small items in the local weekly market: soap, combs, mirrors, mousetraps, flashlights, matches, and the like. He had a bicycle equipped with a big box on the back to transport his merchandise and, now with no farm to go to, he could expand his business by visiting other markets in the area. All told, if you were willing to peddle up to 50 kilometers over path and trail, you could find a market every day and there were always at least a few customers for these basic goods.

So Jerome's family made the big shift. He was off at markets every day. His oldest son, Patrice, now also free of farming duties, left for the biggest city on the coast to move in with a cousin and try his hand at city life. His eldest daughter, Monique, after a lengthy exchange of letters, moved to a largish city in the North where a distant relative had a small restaurant and where she would work as a combination cook-waitress. His other children were still in primary school and would have their routine little changed as they marched the two kilometers to and from school every day. It was really his wife Françoise who had the biggest adjustment to make; a smaller family, no farming, and a husband who was now off in markets every day trying to make a living. Françoise risked having something she had never had before; free time.

Jerome was now gone so much he didn't witness the deterioration of the village. People young enough to do so moved away. The elderly sat in the sun more and died earlier, the extended family was dying with them. With no farms to grow their own food and pitiful few opportunities to have a working wage, families bent and then broke under the weight of the imposed social change. Social bonds strained with the pressure and traditional family values were progressively replaced by an "every-man-for-himself" mentality.

The once thriving village now took on an aura of dreary abandon. The byways and pathways of the hamlet began to sprout weeds as they were less travelled, those houses with thatching suffered a similar proliferation of vegetation. The beaches along the stream where the women washed clothes were now nearly empty and the central press where the wives and daughters extracted fresh palm oil now stood unused as no one had any more oil palm plantations to be able to have the palm kernels to press.

What had been the parade ground and football field in front of the Chief's Palace now housed the beginning of what would be a very large Chinese camp. Here there were long houses of corrugated metal and cardboard that served as the living quarters; a string of parallel necklaces of three-by-four rooms, each housing two technicians or six laborers. Each set of eight rooms had one faucet for water on the narrow veranda that fronted the barracks. There were also large communal latrines and large communal kitchens with woks over a meter in diameter to prepare huge quantities of stir-fried vegetables.

These vegetables, along with whatever meat products the crew consumed, were all raised by the newcomers in farming areas adjacent to the camp. There were few if any contacts with the villagers and no commercial ties; the camp was self-contained and socially isolated, as it wished to be. The plan called for the camp to grow at a rate of about fifty percent a year so, that within five years, there would be six times more Chinese in the shadow of Mount Bapit than there had been farmers in the village.

But, perhaps gratefully, Jerome was outside the goings-on of the Chinese and the Chinese camp. Through no choice of his own, he was no longer a farmer and now a *commerçant*—a merchant, albeit a very small-scale merchant. He had to retool his life, learn new skills, and listen to a new song. But he was up to the challenge and soon had significantly expanded his business and the quantity of small merchandise he was able to sell each week.

But Françoise was less able to adapt, or perhaps had less need to adapt. Her newly discovered free time, first seen as a wonderful and unexpected gift, now became a burden. Jerome left on his bicycle well before dawn, only returning after sunset, exhausted after hours of haggling and peddling. He was just about able to wolf-down a plate of food before falling in a heap on his bed.

Françoise did rise early to make breakfast for Jerome and then to get the younger kids ready for school. But once the children had gone, apart from a small amount of housecleaning and the occasional laundry, time hung heavily on her hands. This free time turned out not to be all it was made out to be.

She began going on walks around the village; visiting friends and acquaintances, seeing family. As the rainy season rolled on into the dry season, and the Chinese built more and more rice paddies, Françoise walked more and more. She was soon going as far as the outskirts of the village where the long thatched palm wine houses were found. Walking in the tropical sun, even in the highlands, can be hot business and the further she went the greater her thirst. Passing the palm wine cabarets was really too much a temptation for a parched mouth and she began to include a cup of palm wine in her daily routine.

These palm wine, or "*mimbo*" bars were typically rag-tag shanties with thatched roofs and often thatched walls. Inside, the dark cubicles had a few rough-hewn benches for the customers and a stool in the corner where the *patronne* would have several large glass jugs filled with wine and a bucket half full of cloudy water where she rinsed the eight-ounce glasses before filling them with the pungent white liquid. Customers could often choose between raffia or "up-palm" wine as well as select freshly tapped wine or "over-night" which had a hydrogen sulfide bouquet, but considerably more kick.

Wine establishments were most often frequented by men, the women guests, aside from the *patronne*, seen as likely to be "free"—hookers by any other name. Françoise's well known position in the village meant she was welcomed and not immediately seen as a sexual object. Nonetheless, her presence made her a visible and potentially available female. For the male clientele, this prospect was worth investing in and they were more than happy to ensure that Françoise's cup was always full.

The dry season wore on and assumed that depressing washed-out look one encounters in the early spring, in some parts of the northern latitudes. All was dry, dusty, and varying shades of dirt-brown. The red clay soil was cracked; the callused heals of your feet were cracked; your skin felt like hundred-year-old parchment;

the walls of houses cracked as the adobe dried; and the streams shriveled with virtually everything desiccated except one's thirst.

These were good times for the *mimbo* houses. The wine was potent, undiluted by rain and bringing top price. Those farmers who had not been displaced by the Chinese, meaning those from nearby villages, were no longer farming as there was no more water. The school year had started so people were no longer saving for school fees and would use whatever little they had to buy necessities like palm wine. Parched throats needed to be appeased and nothing cut a thirst like cool fresh palm wine.

So, as the leaves and flowers dried, Françoise found herself more and more on the benches of the cabaret, drinking more and more due to the generosity of the boys down the bench. But nothing is free and, as was bound to happen, the generous providers began to ask for some compensation. And one day it happened. Jerome had been especially busy and fatigued. Françoise especially fretful and board. The good looking young cattle herder who was just moving through had bought more than enough wine to overcome her inhibitions. When he asked her to join him and go to the *mimbo* house in the next village, she had no problems in accepting. As tactfully planned by the herder, one thing led to another and soon he and Françoise were frolicking in the back room of some-one-or-other's house.

This was the famed step over the line. Almost magically all the males who frequented the various wine dens immediately knew that Françoise was now in fact "free". There was no turning back for her and no looking back for them. It soon became a regular event that she would share her favors with one or more of the customers, who indeed became her customers. While the first fling had been just that, she soon realized the potential profit in these subsequent encounters and found that, like Jerome, she had quite a well-tuned business acumen—only for a different business.

There was no real regret or recrimination. She was able to buy things she had never thought possible: expensive English wax cloth, imported leather shoes, and colorful jewelry. She could even occasionally go to the real off-license bars and buy a beer or a small bottle of cheap red wine; bars where there were also men who would pay much more for the same services she provided the palm wine crew. And, moreover, she was no longer bored.

For Jerome, this transformation of Françoise passed unnoticed. He was fully inundated by his own business. As he did more business, he had to keep more balls in the air. He would go to a village market and unload the box from his bike, carefully laying out all his merchandise in a well-organized and visible manner. He would then sit for six to eight hours on a tiny raffia stool, bargaining with nearly-decided customers, cajoling would-be customers, and trying to snag passers-by. As things were purchased, he replenished his wears on the low bamboo table covered with a plastic sheet, trying to make everything as appealing as possible to his customers; in many ways, unbeknownst to him, very similar marketing strategies to his wife's.

The rains came and went through their timeless cycle before Jerome had the first inkling of the situation, when his Uncle made a very obtuse remark about Françoise's penchant for *mimbo* houses. As a palm tapper, he was an insider on the palm wine scene and had known for some time about his Niece-in-Law's pastimes. But her romping was receiving ever-increasing notoriety and he was concerned that Jerome would ultimately hear of it from a less sympathetic source.

When Jerome innocently broached the subject with her, she unrepentantly acknowledged her vampish habits, coldly announcing that he was too poor to keep her in a lifestyle to which she had now become used and of which she was worthy. Although he no longer had a farm, she declared that he was nothing more than a peasant farmer and would never be more than that. He had no appreciation of the finer things of life and had never realized how lucky he had been to have such an exceptional wife; a wife who was now leaving him for the good life.

Redeeming the good name of his wife was now a moot point. Jerome had no comeback. In the abstract, this was just another of life's setbacks. For, she had been right on target in one way, he was still a farmer at heart and the loss of his farms had been such a tremendous shock that the follow-ups like the loss of his wife were almost anticlimactic.

He had, in fact, seen very little of his wife since he had lost his farms. Now that she was going in search of the good life, she was leaving him and not the reverse. Thus, he didn't have to leave his house or really even change much in terms of his post-farming routine. With surprising lack of emotions, he helped her leave, went to see his Uncle to arrange for one of his nieces to take care of the school-age children, and then went to bed to gain back his strength for tomorrow's long peddle to the market.

Jerome's life seemed to turn round-and-round like the crank on his bicycle. Around and around, but not going very far and often turning up where you started. Sunrise peddling, noon market chaos, sunset peddling. Full moon, crescent moon, mud or dust, around and around. The days melded into a time stream like a muddy river in flood; no real beginning or end, just swirling motion.

His younger children moved through their grades and merchandise moved across his market stalls. Unnoticed by him the Chinese came and came and came, but little rice seemed to follow.

Then one day his Uncle came to see him again, looking very uncomfortable as though he were always the bearer of bad news, and indeed he once again was. Patrice had gone to move in with his son and he now had, like an ill wind, a miserable message to deliver: Patrice was in prison.

All popular images to the contrary, there were few job opportunities in the big cities and those going to find fame and fortune most often found frustration, filth, and failure. Those who did not promptly return to the village frequently ended up on the wrong side of the law; petty thieves, drug dealers, or carjackers. This had been Patrice's lot and he had been captured while trying to break into the house of a police captain. It was not enough that he had proven himself to be a common thief, but a stupid thief to boot—breaking into a police officer's home, how harebrained can you get?

As with Françoise's departure, Jerome accepted the news stoically. A farmer without a farm was like a sailor without a ship. There was no way life could be normal or even tolerable as long as this great void existed. He continued because each day followed the next and it was like drudging up the sides of Mount Bapit in a great deluge; you put your head down and one foot in front of the other and you moved ahead, not ever really looking up to see where you were going.

His one ever so modest pleasure was seeing his younger children grow and develop. Particularly the eldest boy at home, Martin. He had always been bright and inquisitive; the traits now serving him well in school. In the times of previous governments, students like Martin would be assured an education through university and then a cushy job in the civil service. But the new multi-party systems that were called democracies had changed so many things, including access to scholarships for excelling students like Martin. In spite of all the belt-tightening, Martin might still squeak by with a bit of luck. He had done very well in the secular state-run primary school; very well. His enthusiasm for learning had caught the attention of the Headmaster of a parochial secondary school not far from the district offices. The Headmaster had offered Martin what amounted to a free ride for a first-class education at a location that was not too far from home; a rare and welcome smile from the gods.

Jerome did not seem to think of the gods or God very much anymore, as their place seemed to have been taken by the Chinese. The village was about half-half: Moslem-Christian. The two faiths coexisted in complete harmony, sometimes one family having members following each religion, especially older unmarried women who changed from their childhood Christianity to Islam as they felt they had more chances being asked to join polygamous Moslem households than being asked to be a first Christian wife at the old age of 35.

The calls to the Mosque on Friday or the Catholic Church on Sunday, as Catholicism was the major denomination, were the same for Jerome. He heard both from the hard, blister-provoking seat of his bicycle; to add insult to injury, a Chinese-made bicycle. Markets in the area were on a seven- or eight-day calendar and were held regardless of the religious events taking place at the same time. So, Jerome was "making market" seven days a week, fifty-two weeks a year.

Jerome was not only oblivious to religious life, but to life in the village in general. He was more of a visitor in his own house than a head-of-household. His Niece took care of the basics, he ensuring she had whatever money was necessary to keep people fed, clothes mended and washed, and school or medical fees paid. When he peddled down the path from the house before sunrise, he could pretend the village was as it used to be since all was cloaked in darkness. The same illusions accompanied his return, so he really had no idea of what changes had been evoked by the Chief's catering to the politicians and the Chinese.

Had he lingered around the village, he would have found it to be a ghost town peopled by the old and the very young, being slowly consumed by an ever-growing Chinese camp. The rice fields were growing even faster than the camp of the people who plowed them. They now occupied the entire plain, all the old village farms, the middle slopes of Mount Bapit, and the valley above the plain. Kilometers of paddies but surpassingly, nary a sack of local rice in any of the markets Jerome frequented.

But Jerome did not linger and all this was unnoticed. His life was a cloud of persistent depression that surpassed anger or even despair. He floated from day to day and market to market in a daze like a sleepwalker, who had some latent or subliminal thoughts, that one day they would wake up and find all this to be a dream. However, the dream did not end, the daze continued and the incessant peddling seemed never-ending. The seasons changed and the only bright spot was Martin's outstanding performance in school and the now strong likelihood that he would be able to get a scholarship for university with the help of the Jesuits.

As one of the seasons changed, his Uncle made another appearance late one evening when he had only just had time to repack his bicycle for the next morning's early departure and hurriedly but gratefully consume a piping hot plate of maize meal and bitter-leaf soup. Uncle's face was even longer than usual and his frown cut deeply into the corners of his cheeks. If his occupation as a wine tapper was not enough to ensure him a pronounced place in the village information network, the fact that his wife was the village gossip did guarantee that he was always among the first to get any news, particularly that which was salacious or slanderous in nature.

Uncle was a noble man and did not arbitrarily nor quickly pass on the sordid and often questionable tidbits he heard from his wife and the *mimbo patronnes*. But, when these matters were of significance to the family and had the air of being probable, as had been the case with Françoise's cavorting, he preferred being the emissary to avoid the garnishing and crass exaggerations that were likely to come from allowing messages to flow through the very active rumor mill.

Thus, he was feeling obliged but most unhappy as he visited Jerome with yet more bad news about Françoise: she had AIDs. It was probably inevitable. Her changed lifestyle made her a prime target and her luck had now run out, she was HIV positive, apparently some of her long-time partners were already dead from the disease. The end seemed all too clear and unavoidable.

As with all the preceding calamities, Jerome took this news showing no emotion. In spite of his bone-aching fatigue, after he saw Uncle off, he drudged up the path to the home of Françoise's Mother to make sure she knew the news and at least had a sympathetic shoulder to cry on.

Françoise's family had been among the leaders of the Christian community. Her father had been a Deacon in the church, being very involved in all activities undertaken by the Catholics. He had been a kind, big-boned man with great empathy for the trials and tribulations of his friends and neighbors. He had been much loved and greatly missed when he died at a relatively young age from an unknown affliction that distended his stomach, labored his breathing, and led to pernicious diarrhea.

Françoise's Mother had, however, not shared in the love imparted on her spouse. She was only surpassed by Uncle's wife as a tattletale, and she had a cruel and vindictive manner that seemed to poison all she did or said. With characteristics that undoubtedly affected Françoise's choice of life paths, she felt herself superior to everyone and mistreated by having to suffer the depravations of village life. In short, she was not a very nice person and everyone knew this and treated her accordingly. But she would now lose someone who, as a daughter, had been much closer to her Mother than she had been to her husband. Françoise's Mother always saw her daughter as a Cinderella in-waiting with Prince Charming just around the corner, coming to take her beautiful daughter away from the drudgeries of the village and to the bright lights of high society in the big cities. Now her destiny was an unpainted eucalyptus box interred in the front yard.

Being in no way the stoic her son-in-law was, Françoise's Mother wailed, screamed, and flailed the air. She shrieked to the skies and their gods, she pummeled the ground and its devils, then railed against mankind before falling prostrate on her stoop. Jerome passively observed the spectacle from start to finish, then went home to bed to get some sleep before the fast approaching dawn.

Monique came home for her Mother's funeral. She was pregnant with a Gendarme's child and announced they would marry in the coming months. He was a Northerner and it was unlikely Monique would be able to make frequent visits home. Her husband-to-be had five other wives and Monique, as the youngest, would end up being responsible for most of the household chores.

Jerome took the news of the effective loss of his daughter in typical fashion. Adding this to the basket of woes he carried every day, he went back to his market stall in a daze.

The days, weeks, and months continued to flow by. Market days came and went. His remaining children slowly migrated to other places and other people. He remained in his old house, or at least he slept in his old house between markets. All was a blur.

Then one day, after an especially difficult ride home via a mud and stone filled path, Jerome received another visit from his Uncle. But this time Uncle's smile covered his whole face and had an amazing spring in his step for a gentlemen of a certain age.

For once Uncle was ecstatic. He could finally come to his sad nephew with some good news, something that could possibly drag the once outgoing and cheerful man out of his shell of sorrow and back into the land of the living. Uncle's younger brother had been somewhat of an anomaly in the family. In a culture of quick marriages and plentiful children, his brother had remained spouseless and childless. As a hard-working young man, he had moved into the Nkam Valley to the south and slowly built up a considerable coffee and vegetable farm. Through perseverance, his younger brother had created a profitable operation that was the envy of all. But, his younger brother had suddenly passed away after a lightening attack of cerebral malaria. And, he had left no successor.

Uncle had just received word that the Nkam farm would be formally ceded to him with the settlement of his younger brother's estate. But he was now far too old to move and undertake the tough job of keeping the farm profitable. This was a perfect opportunity for Jerome, businessman and farmer, the ideal choice to take over management of the Nkam farm.

When Uncle made his offer to Jerome, Jerome looked at him as though he were an apparition. At first Uncle thought Jerome had finally broken, the stress had been too much and his mind had snapped. Then, like someone awakening from a dream, Jerome's eyes focused for the first time in what seemed like eons and he whispered to his Uncle; "I again hear the farmer's song".

Zoé's Desire

SHE WAS ONE OF many. She was teetering on that threshold of transitioning from being a girl to a young lady. She was in her early twenty's and this was neither old nor young, this was a good thing. Like the hundreds of similar females with whom she shared the streets and byways of the provincial capital, she was a product of the village. Her life had started as the lives of hundreds of thousands of village girls. When she had been old enough to bear the weight, she had carried her younger brother on her back as her pregnant Mother worked the fields. As her strength grew, she carried brimming head-pans from the stream to the house and bundles of wood from the mountain to the kitchen. As she continued to grow, she soon was part of the family team that went to the fields every morning with hoe or machete in hand and a basket on her head to bring back the cassava or sweet potatoes for the evening meal. It was a grueling sunrise to sunset existence, but an existence filled with the carelessness of youth and the happiness of family and community. It was not only hoeing, carrying, and drudgery. It was swimming in the stream, climbing the mango trees, playing hide-and seek in the forest, and running across the savannah. It was many things. It was a celebration of life.

But as a girl grows in the village, all is not family and household chores. There is church on Sunday with prayer and psalm singing on Wednesday. And, when you are old enough, there is school. For some, the village's school may not seem like much. It was a long shed with half-walls of mud-block and a zinc roof, subdivided into six rooms for the different primary classes. Each room had a piece of old plywood painted with blackboard paint on the front wall along with several rows of rough wooden benches. The higher grades actually had makeshift desks to accompany the benches. It was probably not much, but it was all they had; and the elders in the village remembered well when they did not even have this, so they were proud their children could have some sort of education.

In fact, the problem was much less the structure itself than finding teachers to teach in the structure. There was a general shortage of teachers in the country and an acute shortage of good teachers. Educators with an established track record could pick and choose, and they very rarely picked or chose rural village schools. Thus, those who came were far from the pick of the crop; often young men who had just finished teachers' college and hoped that a few years in the village would springboard them to better positions in the cities. So they accepted rural appointments, poor infrastructure, low salaries, and no health care; to get their feet on the first step of their careers.

But there were unpublicized secondary benefits. Teachers, even very young and inexperienced teachers, were considered as "intellectuals" by the villagers. This accorded them an automatic leadership role that was almost parallel to that of the priest or the village chief. Partly due to the respect of the position, and partly because village people are by nature generous and open, there were also great benefits to be reaped from the village's hospitality.

Even those who had so little to eat themselves always shared with the teachers and the village mentors never went hungry. They were always invited to village celebrations. They were greeted with open arms and received so much, but often gave so little.

Zoé had been ecstatic when she had been able to go to school. The long walks to and from school in the early mornings and late evenings were no barrier to her enthusiasm for learning. The often meal-less lunch breaks and draconian discipline, including hard wraps on the knuckles with a heavy wooden ruler or crawling on the sharp gravel on hands and knees around the schoolhouse; could not dampen her hunger for knowledge and her joy at being amongst her classmates.

She excelled in her classes, frequently getting eight or nine out of ten. When she got home, she sat on a stool near the hearth in the kitchen behind the house and, as her Mother stirred the maize meal, she recounted each detail of the day's studies. After doing her evening chores she crowded around the kerosene lamp with her brothers and sisters and scratched her homework with a nub of a pencil. The sixteen-hour days were filled with pleasure: the pleasure of learning; the pleasure of friends; the pleasure of family.

The weeks rolled into months and the months into years. The routine changed little. School, home, and a few cherished minutes of play merged into a pattern that was repeated as Zoé had moved from class to class.

Although the routine remained nearly constant, her body did not. Her little girlish roundness gave way to a womanly shapeliness with budding breasts and well-defined hips. Her girlfriends underwent similar metamorphoses and were filled with wonder as they had watched the changes.

Indeed, it was not only the girls who marveled at their growing maturity. Although most of the boys in the class were still hormonally behind the girls and preferred a football in the school-yard to thoughts of lust and debauchery, the young teachers were certainly not beyond being tempted by this fresh fruit. Some of the less scrupled among them carefully planned ways of having the most buxom among the girls feel threatened with failure and then magically changing their fortunes with only a slight reciprocation in a back room or a nearby shed.

Zoé's excellence with her studies put her outside the reach of such trickery by her teachers although her ripening body certainly did not put her out of reach of their fantasies. They tried to entice her with clothes or even money but she consistently resisted. She demonstrated a surprising ability to maintain both her grades and her virginity.

But all this changed when the handsome young Frenchman came to the village. Later, people would accuse Zoé of racism, of refusing to lower herself by sleeping with someone from the village, and "keeping herself" for a foreigner. This was, she knew, completely untrue. She never planned to sleep with any one, villager or foreigner. None of this ever entered her mind. It just happened.

The Frenchman was posted to the district headquarters, an agronomist who was to help villagers grow a new strain of disease-resistant coffee. He travelled to the various villages in the district and organized workshops and set up demonstration plots. Completely by chance the demonstration plot chosen for her village was part of her Father's farms.

The Frenchman came every fortnight to monitor the coffee stand and help with the new nursery. He would set a semi-circle of chairs and stools near the chosen plot and invite any of the farmers to come and ask questions. Out of curiosity, Zoé tried to attend these impromptu sessions, hanging in the background in the shade of the avocado tree and observing the questions the farmers asked, as well as the answers the Frenchman gave. Her focus often changed from the topic under discussion to the discusser. Were white people really the same as they were? He looked the same, but he was, after all, the first white person she had seen up close. But all the outward signs seemed to indicate they were quite like the people of the village; two arms, two legs, two ears, different hair, but that was too bad. And that skin. She had thought that white people were white. But this specimen was far from white. His skin had the color of the grasses of the savannah during the dry season, a brownish-yellow. Certainly not white.

One day, as she watched from the security of the avocado tree, Zoé sneezed. She sneezed right at the moment when there had been a hush between a question asked by one of the farmers and the answer given by the Frenchman. It had not been a very big sneeze, really quite dainty, but it sounded to her like the roar of thunder; and was obviously loud enough to catch the attention of the Frenchman, who turned in her direction and smiled, quite a charming smile. Embarrassed by her feeling of being the uncomfortable center of the group, Zoé fled to the banana stand where she hid from her unfortunate embarrassment.

She was leaning against a clump of banana trees, hyperventilating when she sensed she was not alone. She turned sharply to find the Frenchman at her shoulder. He assured her that he had followed her only to reassure her not to be afraid of him, but the damage had been done, once their eyes had met, the Frenchman seemed dumbstruck. He immediately felt Zoé as a presence; a true kind and generous, if naive, spirit housed in a gorgeous and succulent body.

For her part, Zoé just continued hyperventilating. She had no idea of what this man wanted, nor why he followed her. But, though charming, she did not feel at ease with a foreigner who, if nothing else, was so much more sophisticated than she.

Irrespective of Zoé's feelings, and in fact quite unbeknownst to her, she had truly smitten the Frenchman and he began to contrive how he could see more of her. The fact that she was young enough to be his daughter was not even a consideration. She was beautiful and full of life. He had felt he must have her.

The Frenchman rescheduled his work plan and began visiting the village every week. He began paying extra attention to Zoé's Father's farm to be able to establish a close relationship with the man; hoping that, with traditional village hospitality, he would soon be invited to the house where he could really evaluate this young female who so attracted him.

His strategy worked perfectly and he was soon a frequent visitor at the home where he joined the family in a mid-day meal of maize meal accompanied by wine and meats that he brought with him. He presented Zoé, her Mother, and sisters with imported English fabric. He brought her Father a milk goat from a new experimental strain that was still not generally available; a huge status symbol for the simple farmer. Flattery turned into almost blatant bribery as the Frenchman prepared to make his move.

He then struck with such finesse that no one could find fault in his proposal. As several of the young village girls had become pregnant, due to encounters with the teachers and had had to drop out of school, Zoé's parents had unquestionable concerns about the future of such a stunning girl as their daughter. The Frenchman offered a solution to their worries. She could come to the district headquarters with him. He would provide accommodation and she could study there free of the intimidation of the young village teachers.

It might have been an exaggeration to say, when Zoé had been informed by her Father that she should kindly accept the Frenchman's offer, she had to be led away kicking and screaming. But, she had certainly not accepted this decision with any of her accustomed gaiety. She was unhappy. Nevertheless, her Father was insistent; the new motorcycle offered by the Frenchman not mentioned in the discussion.

Zoé loved her village and her family and had no desire whatso-ever to go away; in her mind, the young teachers posed no threat. Her desire was, in fact, to spend her life in the village and follow in her Mother's foot-steps, becoming a farmer's wife, a person of the land, and a member of a strong community.

However, these were times when a daughter, or even a son, did not countermand a Father's wishes. Adults in general and leaders in particular, including parents, were to be respected and obeyed. Zoé felt a keen responsibility to follow these norms and follow her Father's instructions, be they ever so far away from her own choices in life. So, unhappily but dutifully, she entered the Frenchman's 404 on that sunny Sunday afternoon and left the village.

Arriving at the Frenchman's house, she was initially filled with a type of fearful excitement at seeing so many new and wonderful things; flush toilet, indoor shower, gas cooker, electric lights, fantastic plates, dishes and kitchen utensils, unusual and unfamiliar beds and bedding, and so much more. From the big things to the little, she experienced a whole new lifestyle.

She was given her own room for the first time in her life, a small converted storeroom in the rear of the house. She used a bathroom shared with the guest-room. She had her own closet with a selection of used clothes the Frenchman found for her.

There was a considerable learning process; new school, new house, new ways of doing things, and almost a new language. She had spoken her Mother's tongue nearly all the time in the village, but learned French in school; so she had a modest grasp of this convoluted dialect.

In spite of the initial strangeness, after a few months she became well entrenched in a new routine, enjoying new studies, and making new friends. She made great progress at learning the "white-man's" ways. The Frenchman said she was like Pygmalion. She had no idea what this meant.

She continued to excel in her studies, to the great satisfaction of her family whom she saw at least once a month. These scholastic achievements seemed to mitigate the feelings they had that somehow she was being indentured.

When all seemed to be going smoothly, her life with a new, but agreeable cadence, the house gods appeared to upset all. One night, the Frenchman came to her room long after she had fallen asleep. He shamelessly removed his clothes and joined her in her bed, awakening her with his caresses and soft words. She was shocked. She had no idea what to do or what he was doing. But he was her benefactor and she had a duty to be respectful to him in his own home. His caresses took on increasing urgency and soon he was showing her how to do things she never imagined a human could or would do.

In the aftermath, she felt nothing. Whatever happened was seemingly most satisfying to the Frenchman and not unpleasant for her. But, at that time, she had not seen it as a life-changing event. It was more like going to Communion—something you did because someone asked you to, but you were not really sure why it was done.

The Frenchman was certainly not so indifferent about the event and he apparently saw it as the beginning of a new relationship with Zoé where, as he had planned, he would no longer be the godfather, but now the lover. His visits to Zoé's room became more frequent and soon he insisted she move into his room and his bed; the seduction now complete.

On one of her monthly visits home, she talked with her Father about the Frenchman's new role. She was very uncomfortable with this and felt it was best for her to find other arrangements; either alternative accommodation in town or to come back to the village. But, her Father saw his daughter as a *nouvelle française* in lovely robes, a splendid house, and plenty of money; enough to generously share with him and the rest of the family who remained stuck in the village. He encouraged her to stay the course and take full advantage of this once-in-a-lifetime opportunity that was due to God's Blessings and for which she should be eternally grateful—to shun such an opportunity would truly be a sin against God and His Goodness.

Zoé's fate seemed sealed and her place in the Frenchman's bed her destiny. For some time, other than the nearly nightly disturbances, these new arrangements did not have any major impact on her routine. School, chores, and monthly home visits continued as always. Then, of course, the inevitable happened. She noticed her "monthlies", to which she was just getting accustomed, did not come one month. She discussed this with her Mother on her next visit to the village and, to her absolute stupefaction, was informed that this meant she would soon be a mother herself.

This was the beginning of a terrible series of events that made her think she was being punished by God for some unknown sin. As soon as she began to "show", she had to leave school. She suffered greatly from her pregnancy to the complete indifference of the Frenchman who continued to seek her affections for as long as he could.

When her baby boy was born, her maternalistic instincts overran her trepidation and she welcomed this new part of her by giving fully of her heart and mind. Although the Frenchman was uninterested in the child, his ardor remained unflagging and he was more than eager to entice her back into his arms.

With surprising rapidity, the inexorable end point was again reached and she found herself with child a second time before their son celebrated his first birthday. The second time around she suffered less and was better prepared to receive their second son. True to form, the Frenchman showed uncut dispassion toward his sons, but was seemingly dedicated to making a third baby as quickly as possible.

Fortunately, these conjugal meetings had been less fruitful and she was able to devote nearly all her time to her sons. Not only were their relations less prolific, but they gradually became less frequent and less enthusiastic, at least on the part of the Frenchman.

He had seen his plan to fruition. He had had his young trophy wife and fathered his sons. End of story, time to move on.

He refocused his attention on a young school girl he had seen in another village and soon prepared his plans for her as, simultaneously, he prepared to have Zoé leave. He thought of a myriad of tales to spin for Zoé, but at the end of the day he had neither the patience, nor the will, to enact these. Ultimately, and very unceremoniously, he simply ordered her to leave with her sons.

In another time and another place, Zoé would have revolted, going immediately to the police to lodge an official complaint against the Frenchman as he had violated her as a minor. But her strong culture of family responsibility and honor combined with her beliefs in predestination, and a strong dose of fatalism, made her accept her lot and go back to the village, with her sons in tow.

The fact that she had children and was not married was really a non-issue for the village. While the community held very strong views on fidelity, chastity was not really a prevalent concept; things happened and youth was, by nature, impulsive. It was not uncommon for someone, married or otherwise, to come back to the village and to rely on the extended family for one or another services, much as the other members of the family knew they too had this privilege. Aunts raised nieces, brothers accommodated younger siblings, grandparents gladly took care of young offspring; the family truly did function on a much larger scale that provided a variety of security nets as well as social and psychological crutches.

Her parents had been nonplussed by her return. Things happen. They had had high hopes and great expectations, but one would not dwell on the past.

The community held no grudge, not referring to her first choice as a foreigner and not one of their own. She too was one of their own and she was now back.

Zoé resettled in her family home. Her boys had the run of the village under the watchful eyes of many. She helped her Mother around the house and her Father in the fields. She eagerly assisted her younger brothers and sisters with their lessons and had long talks with her older family members. She established a new routine that was somehow quite similar to the one she had had before the Frenchman had come into her life, without any schooling of course, and life went on.

But, as she had heard the Frenchman's colleagues often say: "you can't go home". Everything was the same and, at the same time, everything was different. She saw and sensed things differently. It was not the lack of the comforts of electricity or indoor plumbing that made the difference. The difference was in her head. Life was just different. She felt as though she had one foot stuck in one world and the other in another.

While her new awareness set her on edge and made her unable to fully settle into the "old" ways, her sons thoroughly enjoyed their days and nights in the village. At the same time, they were having a much higher quality of life than they would have had in the tumultuous household of the Frenchman.

After months of trying, Zoé made her decision. As distressing as it was, she left her sons with her parents and went back to the other world, to see if she could adapt better there. And so it was.

She did not want to have the slightest chance of meeting the Frenchman. So she chose to try her "other-worldly" legs in the provincial capital. And here she now was, with her "sisters" on the city streets.

Things, of course, had not worked out as she wished. When she first arrived in the big city, she had planned to find a job and go back to school. She was able to find a low-paying job as a server in a bar, but was quickly made aware of the reality that there was not any chance of getting back into school. Even for those of more a typical school age, those who had not lost so much time as she had due to her two pregnancies; there was a long waiting list. Only those children whose families were able to come up with a considerable cash incentive were able to actually take classes. With no family backstopping, she had virtually no chance of ever achieving her desire and resuming her education.

Putting up with the bar job was nearly as frustrating as not being able to go to school. The pay was low, the hours long, and the harassment unending. To the drunk and nearly-drunk, any female in the bar was fair game, and her good looks and youngish age made her a highly sought-after target.

As the days followed one the other, whether due to hormones or boredom, or out of shear sport, she began occasionally to reciprocate to the attentions of selected better-behaved customers and rapidly found the gratuities she received were far, far more generous than her meagre stipend paid by the bar's owner.

The scales really tipped when she moved in with a friend to share rent. Her roommate was a nurse at the public hospital and received only slightly more than Zoé in her bar job. What's more, she worked even longer hours and was more harassed by a wider range of people from doctors to the sick themselves. Clearly education and training made little difference when one was a single female. The two exasperated ladies decided they would have to join them to beat them. They used their small savings to buy some up-scale clothes and began frequenting the few high-quality hotels and bars in the city to look for well-to-do clients.

At first they were more ill at ease with their peers than their would-be customers. Their haunts were patronized by a veritable crowd of girls; girls of all descriptions from hard-core hookers and village just-arrived to teachers who needed extra income, and wives who needed a change from dumb-drunk spouses. There were the sophisticated and the simple, the avarice and the humble, the apt and the ill-adept—they were all there.

This pursuit was not like the whoring she had heard the Frenchman and his friends talk about. This was not a business, with all comers welcome, as long as the agreed-to compensation was met. This was more like playing the lottery. It was a bizarre mix of fantasy, socializing, and livelihood. The girls would sit together, chatting and drinking whatever they could afford while the customers would come and go. If there was music they would sometimes dance. They would sometimes share a table or bar stool. It was understood the man would pay for a drink and they would talk. At times this would lead to the bedroom and at times it would lead nowhere. For most, there was no negotiation, but more a selection based on first reactions; who liked whom. It was also understood that some form of compensation, at the man's discretion, was normal. There was unquestionably a financial side to the arrangements, but these were often more than counterbalanced by the social aspects.

Zoé was lucky. Helped by her youth and beauty, she had no problems picking and choosing those with whom she wished to be and these gentlemen were always more than generous. While not the life she had envisioned when she was carrying her little brother on her back in the village, life could certainly be worse.

One serene evening at the beginning of one of the endless chains of weeks, Zoé was sitting calmly in a quiet bar with an older woman, whom she had frequently seen around. The older lady was, what would have been called, an experienced woman. She had seen it all and survived. She and Zoé exchanged tales as they slowly sipped their sodas. At one moment, unexpectedly the older woman asked Zoé to describe her desires for her life.

Since her school days, she dared not think in this direction. She had had desires, hopes, and expectations. Now, she only had, she hoped, tomorrow. Desire, what did she now desire, now that she had abandoned her sons, entered a foreign world, and changed—oh, how she had changed.

But her elderly companion pursued the topic and insisted on knowing Zoé's desires.

It was hard. Like the proverb said, "you can't bend a dried fish". But she forced herself. What did she want? What could she want? It was too much. There was so much to want and so little to realistically expect. Her comrade pushed the point. She must reply. And then, like the first fringes of pink on a dawn sky, the answer came: she wanted to be in her Uncle's mango tree, high above the ground, eating a sweet, fresh, tree-ripened mango with the juice running down her chin. Yes, that was a worthy desire. Then she felt a tap on her shoulder as someone asked her to dance.

The Manipulator

POISON WAS ALWAYS THE cause, whenever someone unexpectedly died. Everyone always blamed poison. This was nearly synonymous with *juju* or some kind of mysterious or black magical
intervention. Nicole saw it as ironical, although community values
and family love were often touted as the vanguards of traditional
society, whenever one could not attribute a direct cause of death,
everyone assumed it was poison. The poisoning being motivated
by jealousy—jealousy, the pandemic disease to which she too was
not at all immune.

She knew full-well that more times than not the deceased
had succumbed to any of the multitude of tropical and age-related
diseases that flourished here, as anywhere. Diseases went undiagnosed for years, due to poor health care, and then struck fatal
blows with lightning speed. But, of course, there were those occasions when dire circumstances demanded dire acts and poison was
used. Herbalists and traditional healers had used the roots, flowers, and barks of the forest and savannah for centuries to restore
health or settle debts. Finding the right substance for the job, be it
good or bad, was not difficult.

Nicole knew about difficulty. She had been born on the wrong
side of the gender gap, in a culture where the eldest son inheriting
the whole estate was standard practice. If she had not been skillful
at manipulation, she would have let this gender inequity ruin her
life and become just another harried female. As it turned out, at
no small cost, she was wealthy and dominated the lives of those
closest to her. She was in control.

Her overriding edict was full speed ahead; let no one or nothing stand in your way. There was no question in her mind that the
end justified the means, and the end was her personal aggrandize-
ment. While financial wealth was part of the equation, this was

far more a question of standing. Wealth brought status and she needed to be the top; not on top, the top.

While she always had a domineering and beguiling personality, she was never able to be outstanding in her own right. She had neither exceptional intellect, athleticism, nor beauty. She was, in fact, quite common and unimpressive. But, she was driven. She was totally devoted to herself and seeing herself in the spotlight. She was also completely amoral, which facilitated doing whatever needed to be done.

Her nondescript childhood had turned into an equally non-descript youth. She remained, at best, average. She had no social life growing up, aside from those purely cosmetic arrangements her Mother had organized. She was incapable of being a friend, thus had no friends. She was unable to love others other than herself, so she had no lovers.

More than being her Mother's daughter, she was her Grand-mother's granddaughter. Although her Mother affected all the guises of a conservative conventional housewife, she had, unlike her Daughter, a well-hidden liberal streak that provoked inner feelings of empathy, equity, and love of one's fellow man. Perhaps surprisingly, but not out of character, her Grandmother needed no affectation and was the true conservative, dare one say ultracon-servative, that fit well the stereotype of the female in the smallish rural community. Like her Grandmother, Nicole abhorred all that was outside her view of the norms. The two ladies, separated by a generation, shared an unswerving view that the world should be as they wanted it; all deviation from this "norm" simply wrong.

Nicole was a hard worker, but a bad student. She was a per-fectionist who perfected nothing. She was intolerant and brutish with the single-mindedness of a charging Cape buffalo. There was no discussion, there were no alternatives. There was her way or no way. She was vindictive and absolutely without remorse or scruples. Her way led in one direction and with one set of rules. You could join her, one step behind, but you could never cross her.

Nicole was not perhaps jealous in the classic sense. She did not covet those things others had and she did not. Coveting implied these were things that were out of reach and Nicole would not accept that anything was out of reach. By one means or another, she was sure of her ability to get to the top. But she was jealous of others, not for what they had, but for the ease with which they greeted life; apparently, not as she, finding it necessary to scheme and fight for each day. This made her bitter; a bitterness that covered a deep undercurrent of envy.

Nicole was, in fact, not a nice person. Nonetheless, her parents, of course, loved her with that blind love only parents can have. She was born shortly after their marriage with her siblings coming much later. Thus, she was nearly a single child, which fit well with her single-mindedness.

When she reached the age at which all respectable young ladies must begin finding a husband, she found she had a storm in her guts and nothing in her heart. She had lived almost a cloistered life with her parents; only venturing out into the world of her peers under extreme duress from her Mother. As a result, she had no social skills and no idea of how to behave toward the opposite sex. She even had very little awareness of her own sexuality.

In the place of those emotions she should have had, she only had insatiable ambition to be the top. In her view of the universe, she herself did not have to be "the top". If one of her offspring gained the pinnacle, she had won. She could achieve her aim surreptitiously. She could, and now seemingly must, reach the top vicariously.

However, even to achieve her goal through surrogates, she needed a husband, In spite of her social ineptness, she needed a husband not only to keep up the appearances of being among the respectful few, but most importantly, to produce with her those offspring who would vault to "the top".

Whether through dumb luck or careful planning, she found someone even more woebegone than she; someone with fewer social skills, equally non-existent friends, comparatively mediocre academic performance, and a dysfunctional but established family—the perfect spouse who would provide children, a good name, and sheepishly stay out of the way. Most critically, someone who she was able to convince needed her and would bend to her every whim.

Her schemes nearly hit a glitch when her parents took an almost immediate dislike to her husband-to-be, feeling their aging dog had more personality than her chosen mate. But they also realized time was not on their side. Nicole was, from the point of view of most eligible bachelors, not all that great a catch.

It was important for Nicole to keep her parents on her side and, as much as possible, unaware of her plans and expectations. Nearly three decades of commonness had had the effect of dampening their own expectations. They were more than happy to see her settle into the role of housewife and mother, if she could just find a better partner. But Nicole was able to make the sale and keep them on the team.

Her game plan was complex and far-reaching as only someone who has so conscientiously devoted all her energies to such a topic can master. While her parents were far from the aristocracy, nor were they landed gentry, they were staunch and respected members of the community with exemplary social position and a solid financial base. They had the standing and the resources necessary for her to achieve, through her ever-changing manipulations, her unchanging goal—to be the top.

When she had her first child, the bonds with her parents were cemented. They were enamored at being grandparents and, when holding their baby grandson, their misgiving about their Daughter's situation melted away. They were now genuinely content with their Daughter and the life she had established and created. Just to make sure the bonds were unbreakable, she soon had a second child and her parents were equally overjoyed with their first granddaughter.

Her parents under control, she had to deal with her siblings. Although she was nearly a decade older than her nearest sibling, she did have four younger brothers and sisters. These fledglings had no idea of her crusade and would not have understood, had they been aware. Sadly, or perhaps not, they were just regular kids who went to school, played football, climbed trees, swam in the creek, and chased cows. They had no crusade. They were not driven. But, they were also not common; each had his or her own areas of excellence. In the aggregate they could overshadow her and her plans. They were a threat. They could attract the attention of their parents, and she could not share the limelight. Her brothers and sisters needed to be dealt with dispassionately and effectively.

So, while she caressed her parents' egos, goaded her Husband, and shielded her children, she mounted a propaganda campaign against her brothers and sisters. This turned out to be easier than she had imagined. Youth always engages on the margins, committing all sorts of errs, while bending to the breaking point most rules and regulations. It was really quite a simple matter to ferret out these miscalculations committed by her siblings; quickly calling the most sever of these infractions to the attention of her parents. When one or another would be disciplined in school, fail an exam, not do homework, disturb a neighbor, or discombobulate the priest; Nicole was sure to find out and even surer to embellish the event as she recounted it to her parents, bemoaning the fact that her own brothers and sisters were so strong-headed, difficult to raise, and a blotch on the family reputation.

Like building a house one brick at a time, her campaign ultimately succeeded as her parents were made aware of the growing body of evidence pointing to the undisciplined and apparently incorrigible nature of the family's youngest children. Slowly but surely she was able to make the needed theatrical presentations to her parents, proving without doubt that she alone, with her own children of course, was worthy of their support.

Her schemes were quite unexpectedly rocketed forward by a totally unforeseen event; the death of her Father. This was a windfall; an incalculable opportunity.

Her parents had been completely in love and dedicated to each other, having grown up together and passed nearly their entire lives as one. With the loss of her Husband, Nicole's Mother was devastated beyond words—lost in a world she no longer understood, nor cared to understand. Enter Nicole the Rock, the solid daughter upon whom Mother could lean and rely.

Nicole now had her Mother in the palm of her hand.

Nicole's hand also now had no small amount of cash in it, as she would be able to assume the management of her Mother's substantial wealth. By burying one person, she had significantly advanced her agenda and her resources. The road to the top was now open.

However, there was one slight bump in the road. Ironically, in spite of all the criticisms she had so vehemently raised of her siblings, her own children were turning out to really be the incorrigible ones. They had inherited their parents' antipathy for school and learning as well as their social fragility. Her children were common.

Ever the planner, Nicole quickly had the answer: another child. She produced another infant as soon as she could and, although female, the child more than lived up to her expectations. This baby was talented and exceptional. This baby grew into a girl who was an outstanding singer, dancer, student, and athlete. It was almost as though all the skills and abilities lacking in the rest of her family, herself included, were personified in her youngest Daughter. This was absolutely someone who would carry her Mother to the top.

Nicole now concentrated all her energies on this young girl; molding her, ensuring that every thought or deed that came from the youngster had been formed by the mother, and was something for which the mother would receive due credit. This little girl was her loadstar, her god *Elegua* who would guide her to the pinnacle.

Nicole knew she was no longer common because she was the Mother of her most uncommon Daughter. She received accolades and kudos from all for the unique jewel that was her Daughter. She aggressively pushed her Daughter to higher and higher heights. Each rung of the ladder her Daughter ascended, the light grew brighter and Nicole felt more and more self-satisfied, completely oblivious to any feelings on the part of this self-same Daughter.

Just when her dreams seemed to be realizable, another potentially damning phenomena arose; her uncommon siblings, despite her denunciation, were becoming successful in their own rights. Her propaganda had been most effective and her parents had withdrawn all but token support from their younger children. Nevertheless, these uncommon individuals had been able to keep their lives together, maturing, and progressing to the point where they were now noteworthy in their own ways; and could unhappily compete with her brilliant Daughter in terms of exceptionalism.

Nicole, as always, reacted to this threat directly from the gut and redoubled her assault on her siblings, becoming more and more vociferous with her Mother about the obvious shortcomings of the other members of her family. While she extolled the virtues of her own Daughter with one breath, with the next she would vilify, in all possible ways, the lives and lifestyles of her siblings; convincing her Mother these ingrates were bringing nothing but shame and rebuke on the honorable family.

For some time, she was successful. While her Daughter successfully scaled the ladder, adding distinction to distinction, her Mother became wrapped up in the little girl's life, becoming an ardent supporter to the exclusion of all other thoughts of family.

But the gods would not leave them in peace and Nicole's siblings doggedly continued their pursuits, seemingly unaware of the threats they posed to Nicole's schemes. Her brothers and sisters became more distinguished, casting shadows that now reached their Mother's doorstep.

Then the pendulum swung and Nicole's Mother began taking heed of her other children, realizing they too were her family, and they too, regardless of the twists and turns presented by Nicole, had not done too badly with their lives. Nicole's Mother began to seek out and re-establish bonds with the rest of her family to the outright panic of Nicole.

At first, Nicole tried what for her was a rather soft touch, repeatedly and vigorously deriding her brothers and sisters for her Mother's benefit. But, most atypically, this strategy backfired and Nicole sensed her Mother was beginning to see a glimmer of light on the horizon, beginning to realize that she had been manipulated, beginning to realize that her emotions had been tricked, much to the detriment of her relations with her other children; these children who were just as much a part of her family as was Nicole. Nicole's Mother once again was becoming the mother of the whole family and the matriarch who would strive for equity among all the family. Nicole's panic turned to dread. Not only could she be toppled from the top, but her Mother's wealth that had helped her get there, and helped keep her there, was now in jeopardy.

Now she was confronted with the real possibility that her Mother would try and share the wealth, not only reducing her assets but, almost worse, sharing them with siblings who had apparently succeeded without scheming and manipulation. This was too much. These were truly dire circumstances.

Nicole had to act. She made some discrete contacts and procured the necessary ingredients. She made her plans with even more care than usual. She felt no sadness at the pending action, indeed she felt nothing; it was an inconvenience and a hurdle that needed to be passed. It was necessary.

She set her plan in motion. When selecting the right time to act, the irony did not escape her when she chose the night of her youngest Daughter's graduation from secondary school. She invited her Mother to an elaborate meal to celebrate the event, where she served a variety of carefully selected tasty tidbits she knew would tickle her Mother's taste buds.

The next day she feigned surprise when she was visited by the priest. Her Mother had unexpectedly passed away in the night, apparently a result of a coughing spell that caused something to be lodged in her throat leading to suffocation. The priest expressed additional consternation regarding the events of the death. Not only was the cause unclear, but Nicole's Mother had seemingly been sitting at the kitchen table at the time of her death. As she had eaten at Nicole's, she was certainly not at the table to eat. Moreover, scattered about her Mother's body were papers and writing materials which proved to be her last will and testament which she had been reviewing or revising. Yet, no revisions were to be found and the documents taken from the table clearly indicated Nicole was the sole inheritor of her Mother's assets.

The road was now open. Nicole could see the top.

A little over a year after Nicole and the rest of the family had laid their Mother to rest, Nicole's younger Daughter had a baby, married the father, dropped out of school, moved to the capital, and became very common. Nicole never spoke to her again.

The Volunteer

HE WAS REALLY NOT at all sure how or why he was where he was, but he was there, where-ever there was. He looked up at corrugated roofing sheets nailed to eucalyptus rafters, the sun dripping through some of the nail holes where the spikes had fallen out before the metal turned red from an accumulation of rust and dust. He looked at the cobwebs in the corners, blackened by cook fires, and at the mortar crumbling from between the mud blocks. His blurry eyes followed the line of blocks from roof to floor, the floor being once a thin sheet of concrete with not much cement or stone, now cratered and cracked from years of abuse. His hands tentatively felt to his left and right, ever so cautiously sensing the surroundings which slowly materialized as a double raffia bamboo bed with a cloth-covered foam mattress and some sort of blanket that was all bunched up in against the wall. As his eyes cleared ever so little, he saw the ill-defined clothes hanging from wooden pegs on the wall, smelled the lingering odor of a kerosene lamp and tasted the foul sewer in his mouth, that raised serious questions as to what he had ingested the night before. This was not a morning like any other, but it was a morning like many others.

Feeling began to return to his extremities, his eyes began to focus as his head began to pound like a gigantic pestle hammering cassava. He finally felt sufficiently alert to be able to swing his feet over the side of the bed and sit up; the cool morning air refreshing his naked torso. While he sat on the edge of the bed, massaging his temples, the crude unpainted wooden door opened and a lady wrapped in a towel entered. It took some serious concentration to recall who she was and the vision that kept returning to his burning mind was that of her seamless face over the top of a beer bottle. Then a name sprang into his brain like a mouse getting snapped in a trap: Charlotte. Or was it Chantal? No, Chantal was in Nkunga and not here, where-ever here was.

She approached the bed with a big smile, an enamel cup of palm wine, and a tin plate of rice and sauce. What more could he want? Perhaps a few answers to the questions of what he had done to end up as he had obviously ended up. But he put on a brave face, gave his benefactor a kiss on her glowing cheek, swallowed a mouth-full of palm wine, and tucked-in.

The palm wine tickled his neurons and the food, heavily laced with hot chillies, made him feel almost among the living. It was as if his blood had started circulating again after having been blocked from reaching his brain for hours. As it surged through his veins, he began to see little speckles of memory fall into place like dust motes from the air.

He was in Palema, the District Headquarters. Yesterday there had been an afternoon meeting of all the district forestry staff to discuss new nurseries to be built as part of a development bank project. He was an agro-forestry volunteer who helped farmers start fruit orchards and plant nitrogen-fixing trees. By mid-morning he had left his village on his motorcycle, his trusted *moto*, to be able to attend the meeting starting after the siesta. The meeting itself had been painless and mercifully short, the DO—District Officer—outlining where and when the new nurseries would be built. By the close of business, he and his forestry colleagues were seriously pounding beers, spending their travel money in the best way they could.

They gaily moved from bar to bar, taking turns at the tab while they snacked on barbecued meat (*soya*), grilled plantains and fish, groundnuts, and roasted fowl. It all would have ended quite differently, probably with an aftermath of just a massive hangover and perhaps a little runny tummy, if he hadn't run across Alfred, a good friend and Gendarme from his village.

Alfred had introduced him to his cousin Charlotte. It seemed Alfred had cousins everywhere.

Alfred and Charlotte joined the group of happy foresters as they continued their celebration of life, with the objective of visiting each of the bars in Palema. Fortunately, the town was not large and this was a doable, if harrowing, task. And, indeed, they had reached their objective and now he was suffering the severe consequences in Charlotte's bed.

Charlotte was very kind and, although hung-over herself, she took pity on her forlorn one-night-stand lover, bringing him a bucket of hot water with which to wash and then another serving of food and drink. By the time he staggered off her rickety porch and onto his *moto*, he was feeling he might be able to actually see tomorrow.

He took the north track out of town. As it was dry season, the road was hard, the rainy season ruts having dried to a consistency of reinforced concrete; all this overlaid by dust—between six and twenty-six inches depending on the road surface. He was about two-thirds through the three-hour trip when he began to feel rumblings in his lower stomach, something akin to storm clouds rolling in rapidly over the horizon. It must have been the palm wine and chilies meeting up with all the concoction of the night; just too much. The rumbles changed into gut-wrenching cramps and he quickly slid to a stop, nearly not getting his bike up on its kick-stand before he headed for the bush, pulling off his jacket and unbuttoning his jeans as he half ran/half hobbled to as isolated place as he could hope to reach before the eruption occurred.

Fortunately, the ever-ready volunteer, he had a ball of toilet paper in his hip pocket and was able to reassemble his affairs and nearly his dignity with minimum adverse effects. All would have, in fact, been really well accomplished had it not been for the old Pa who reared his head from the coffee plantation near the eruption's site and asked "*Massa, how now?*".

Although his motorcycle seat felt the slightest bit squishy after his visit to the coffee farm, the remainder of the trip was uneventful; two near-misses with chickens and one each for goats and pigs.

As he pulled into his village, he had the best intentions to go straight to work, but passing his house he invented the need for a cool class of water as an excuse to stop. Seeing his bed was enough. He fell on the lumpy mattress and did not move until the next sunrise.

The new day was heralded by a new dawn that found him up and ready to get on the road and visit his farmers. There was a great deal to do and he was imparted with a considerable amount of responsibility considering his limited practical experience. As a recent graduate with a bachelor's in biology, he would scarcely qualify as a county expert back home, but here he was actually ran the whole program. He thoroughly enjoyed his work, but his farmers relied on him and he took this very seriously.

He spent the next several months on his usual routine, visiting farmers and government nurseries five or six days a week, partying hard every weekend and at least several times during the week, making the jolting bike trips to his most distant farmers all the more uncomfortable. He would leave his modest abode early every morning, coming back into the village before sunset and stopping off at his favorite bar. On slow days he would have a few beers and some street food before getting home in time to listen to the radio before going to bed. On busy days he would be carousing until close to midnight, sometimes making it home, others waking up in a variety of locales.

The highlight of this period was a very extraordinary weekend he spent with a forestry volunteer from the eastern side of the country who had come for a visit. They started with a little friendly competition to see who could consume the most gin. Then, with the arrival of Alfred, the games turned serious and the night turned to morning. Alfred was found beneath a pre-independence broken-down dump-truck talking with a family of chickens. The two volunteers, though they would never admit it, were rumored to have carried their good-natured competition to the bedroom to see who could practice the most innovative romance with the girls with whom they linked-up during the course of the night. It was also rumored that the climax of this competition was when one chugged a bottle of tequila, seconds later, his eyes rolling to the top of his head and his body in free-fall until it encountered the floor. The conscious of the two thought his good friend was dead.

He immediately wondered how he would be able to explain this to the Volunteer Director. He had spent several hours contemplating wilder and wilder stories to describe how the volunteers had lost one of their own. Finally, he had succumbed to his own libations, dropping to the floor next to his chum. To his great relief, he was revived by his heretofore departed compatriot, this latter enquiring as to where to find a cold beer to "wash his brain"—take *clearance* as the volunteers called it.

As the season's changed, it was time to get the nurseries in shape. Many of the seedlings were produced in the rainy season and the beds had to be prepared well in advance. While the operations of the nurseries themselves were not his responsibility, the setting-up was.

As a first step, along with other forestry staff, he had to meet with officers from the District Office to collate the seedling needs and plan the use of various nursery facilities; subsequently providing the guidance in the raising and distribution of these plants—the work itself carried out by the community. This whole process required several months, even when all went well.

The beginning was a week-long series of important meetings; meetings that affected his farmers. While the evenings were devoted to imbibing, checks were put in place, and he arrived each morning on time for the meetings, and without a hangover, or at least not much of one.

His nearly chaste life was facilitated by the fact that he was lodged at the local Catholic Mission where there was a strict code of conduct and curfew. As the Catholics and the chief civil servants competed for the most prominent plots on the highest hills of the town to build their respective edifices, the meetings at the District Offices were very close to the Mission. He would walk to the offices every morning, passing by the DO's residence and the colonial tennis courts before going to the conference hall at the back of the government compound.

On one morning he was just passing the tennis courts when he caught but a glimpse of a young lady coming from the market at the foot of the hill. She was walking very nobly; straight back and slow, even steps with her market basket at her side. She did not even look at him but somehow he felt there had been an almost intimate connection.

The forestry meetings reached a satisfactory end and he was spending his last night in town with his friend who was an English teacher at the local secondary school. As they were sitting on the veranda having a beer or two, his friend's wife returned from a get-together, a *Njangé* as they called it. She was accompanied by her friend who she introduced as Camille.

He was shocked. Camille was the lady with the market basket he had seen several days earlier. Although she made no acknowledgement of this previous chance crossing of paths, she did greet him with an intoxicating smile and a cool firm handshake. He was finished. Smashed! Camille had him, even though she knew it not.

He returned to his village and his farmers but was plagued by thoughts of Camille. It became an obsession and he finally invented some excuse to travel to the District Headquarters, making a beeline for his friend's house to find out how to get in touch with Camille. He had to know more about her.

This turned out to be easier than he had imagined. The town was small and everyone knew everyone. Camille lived on a little hill on the other side of town from his friend, she shared a room with a roommate. As it turned out, both ladies were from another area about 50 kilometers to the east, but had come to Palema to look for work.

Although never considering himself as being someone endowed with many social skills, he even surprised himself when he found he was able to establish a solid friendship with Camille. Contrary to his typical ways, his intentions were not to get her into bed as fast as humanly possible, but rather to become her friend. Lo and behold, he succeeded and they had several very pleasant evenings together before he returned to his village, promising to come back to see her as soon as possible.

The gods smiled upon him and he was, through a variety of direct and indirect means, able to call upon Camille on a regular basis. As their relationship grew and solidified, he knew he wanted to live with her. But, when he broached the subject, she was always evasive. It was not that she did not like, maybe even love, him. But she had left her home in search of work and bettering her position. She had hopes of being able to continue her education and land a real job, not the part-time ill-paying positions that had kept her going so far. All his arguments failed to convince her to forsake her future path to be with him.

Perhaps solely by trial and error, he finally hit on a formula that seemed to have all the needed elements. He would buy a sewing machine for her and arrange for her to work as an apprentice for a good tailor in his village. This way, should she decide to leave, she would have a sewing machine and a basic trade to fall back upon and help her get established while she tried to arrange for her further education. This worked.

She took her few belonging to his village by taxi and the two set up house together. This was a miracle. Every day they would share breakfast before he went to visit his farmers. In the evening he would come straight home. Sometimes they would spend a quiet evening together, in each other's arms. Other evenings they would go out together, having a few beers and seeing some of his old friends, but keeping things well under control. This was a new and welcome routine. He worked harder and loved harder.

The dry season returned and they joined hands to fight the dryness and drought. Dust everywhere, no water for days, and the sky an irritating brown; dirt seemed to enter every crevice of your body. Albeit very uncomfortable, when they tackled it together it seemed less of a problem and more of an adventure.

With a great gush, the rains then returned and they continued to be happy in their union, finding many more things to rejoice in than to complain about. Their life was surreal. In many ways they were not part of this Earth but only part of each other. There was no past nor any future, only today. There were no countries, oceans, or seas. No families; mothers or fathers, sisters or brothers. There was only now.

But volunteers come on a contract and contracts end. The "now" came to crashing end when the end of the contract reared its ugly head. His time was soon to be up. What would they do?

She had been the reluctant one. She had been the one who had had trepidations about moving in together. While many of her friends would have fallen over backwards to marry a foreigner and leave this poor and struggling country for the good life of the developed world, this thought had never entered her mind. She was her Father's daughter and a daughter of her country. She was where she wanted to be. But now he had entered her life and upset all the equilibria. Now things had changed.

Things had changed for him, too. He had no doubt that he loved her. The old try-everything spirit that had made him become a volunteer in the first place tried to gain the upper hand, convincing him that she was truly a wonderful person and they owed it to each other to continue their relationship in spite of the obvious hurdles of race and culture. They had done too much together, developed too strong a bond, to throw it all away simply because his contract had ended.

However, he also heard another voice. A voice of dissent. A voice that reminded him of how different their races and cultures were. A voice that reminded him that back home, in many areas, such intermingling was greatly frowned upon, even illegal. This voice reminded him that he came from a good solid family, he had a bright future, and could continue his schooling, or enter into the family business; he could do so much, but how much could he do if he were with her?

This was an agonizing time. The battle of the darkness versus the light raged on; yin vs yang. There was no easy path. There probably was no right path. Alas, there seemed to be no path at all.

They talked and talked. He walked and walked. He even drank and drank. But every morning he would wake up and find the same dilemma on his door step. He knew he had only to make the first move and they would leave together to a new life and new adventures. He knew it was possible and with her magnetic personality; they were certain to succeed at whatever they did. But, there was always that nagging "but". He couldn't make the move, he couldn't make the decision.

He entered into his shell for days before his departure date arrived, avoiding any further discussion with her; leaving her totally in the dark as to what lay ahead. He knew full well her thoughts and heart. She knew so little of his. But she knew he loved her and she had confidence, she had faith. All would work out for the best, all would work out as it should.

But he found himself unable to cross this last line. His despair led to desperation. He was ashamed to be circumspect with her, she deserved much better. He was ashamed at being fearful of the future. As he spiraled into the void of uncertainty, he finally chose deception as the only way out.

He told her he had discussions with his service and would be able to extend his contract by a year, thereby postponing this inevitable and difficult decision as to what to do about their relationship. He told her he had to go to the capital to sign the papers for the extension. He told her he would be gone for a few days but when he came back all would be as it had been. He told her many things.

He then took the next plane west, the next flight back to civilization. Back to family and friends. Back to deep roots and deeper traditions. Back to the old, the comfortable, and the secure.

About eight months later Camille had a beautiful little baby girl, Joelle, who had a full hamper of clothes she made on her now almost band-new sewing machine.

Many years later, in 2001, as a highly paid executive, he was working in the World Trade Center on September 11th. He is fondly remembered by his family and friends.

Mr. N'FOUR

PEOPLE OF MY GENERATION have often used epithets to cleverly camouflage what might be considered as less than admirable traits. Someone is "sassy" rather than being undisciplined. Another may be "energetic" rather than simply stating he or she has run amuck. An "exuberant" fellow can't keep quiet; dare I say, won't shut up. This obtuse nomenclature covers all aspects of our lives. However, in some cases it may become more graphic.

Using a more socially acceptable taxonomy may side-step taboos while providing insight into someone's character or behavior. Working in the sawmills of the rural Pacific Northwest, the blasphemy and profanity aside, I learned many colorful adjectives used to describe executives and politicians, as well as fellow workers and their families. The "shepherd" was the foreman who tried to round everyone up; while the "whistler" was the supervisor who was invariably blowing wind through his teeth as he hyperventilated up the stairs.

As with more things than we realize, these titles could often be of a sexual nature. Among the multitude of labels employed in this male-dominated blue-collar mill environment, there were often expressions of women's sexual behavior. As, according to myth, all men are inherently virile and in control of the sexual situation. My colleagues often referred to their obsequious partners as being "moaners" or "groaners" as they climaxed; reportedly brought to this pinnacle by the man's unerring skill and finesse.

All of this lengthy preamble is not intended to be a titillating introduction to a verbal Blue Film on mill-workers' sex-lives, but is simply setting the stage for introducing our neighbor. We recently had occasion to spend an extended stay in a hotel. As in most hotels, architects arrange rooms as mirror images. The head of the bed in the neighbor's room, therefore, separated from the head of our bed by approximately six inches of plasterboard, studs, and paint. We were in Room 2, our neighbor in number 4.

Our neighbor was apparently on some sort of prolonged assignment as it seemed as though he too had arranged for a long-term stay in the hotel. On weekends he would frequently come back from his outings with a female companion and invariably, in the early morning hours, we would be awakened to a series of loud grunts wrapped in a giggle as the bed in the neighboring room massaged the wall as its occupant apparently vented his sexual verve. Our neighbor was a "grunter"—the ladies seemed to be silent partners.

Through our six-inch barrier, we followed the grunter's weekend escapades and soon felt as though we knew him well enough to give him a name; although we had never seen him and did not know his name. So, we named him Mr. N'four in Room 4.

N'four is a surname from western Cameroon and, with great nostalgia for this special land, it seemed a good choice for our unknown neighbor, albeit he was almost certainly not from Cameroon. The Cameroonian connection, however, brought to our minds some commentary regarding how people act and interact; not just in bed.

Cameroonians are among the most sociable of people. They have a culture of being open and friendly. One cannot remain a stranger for very long in Cameroon. Any newcomer will quickly be deluged with queries: "who are you", "where do you come from", "what do you do", "how do you like it here"? In the offices, taxi parks, markets, and where ever more than two people congregate, someone will recognize a stranger and make an overture.

Alas, these attributes are not trans-national and sadly have not become incorporated into the American lifestyle. Quite to the contrary, our society has evolved into an insular and solitary existence where we can "know" someone during their most intimate moments without knowing who they are.

Our Mr. N'four may be a grunter, but he is also symbolic of the thousands of faceless people we encounter. Mr. N'four will float into and out of our lives; in the future all we will remember is

Mr. N'four the grunter. Yet there is unquestionably much more to Mr. N'four, as there is to all of us. We all have a past, present, and future. We all have a sense of self; but, in today's culture, this has been transcended by selfishness. We scarcely have time for ourselves, let alone those who live next to us.

There is at least one real Mr. N'four, a high school teacher from the village of B'kham, in the English-speaking highlands of western Cameroon. Mr. N'four was a son of the village chief and was first in the line of succession. But, contrary to common opinion, the work of a village chief was hard and required great responsibility if it was to be done correctly—the people coming before the palace.

Being a *Fon*, or Chief, is not the life of ease that many observers might expect. Chiefs may seem to have lives out of another age; the very traditional Anglophone tribes often having a *Fon* with a mighty palace, a beautifully carved throne, sometimes even embellished with leopard skins, along with several scores of wives, some very nubile, and much younger than he. Although these leaders spent hours eating and drinking the best their kingdom had to offer, they were also very directly held responsible for the people; adjudicating disputes, arranging family dilemmas, and acting as the Government's interlocutor.

Chiefs received a chicken to settle an argument over ownership of a bunch of plantains and a goat to arrange a quarrel over a wife; but, they had to reach consensus over the plantains and the wife—they really did have to wear the mantle of Solomon. While the Government's civil servants could dexterously come into the kingdom and levy taxes or take a census; they came and went. The Chief stayed.

There are many reports of the people "removing" an ineffective or irresponsible chief. But, since a chiefdom-ship is a life-long appointment, when a bad leader is removed; this can only happen through death. The people do really have power over their leaders.

Our friend, the real Mr. N'four, did not want to be encumbered by the responsibilities of leadership nor worry about mortal failure. He had achieved a high level of education and wanted to

PHOBOS & DEIMOS

use this, while he saw more of the world. Mr. N'four fled B'kham and the palace, going to the Francophone part of the country where he could easily find a job as a high school English teacher.

Mr. N'four quickly integrated into local life. By the time we met him, he had been away from B'kham for more than a decade and had no real intention of returning to open the old wound of his failure to live up to his family's expectations. His Father was now dead and another son had become the *Fon*. For his part, Mr. N'four was happily settled in a new life, in a new place. He was, as he wished, using his education and free of the cloak of responsibility that accompanied the palace and all the palace wives. Mr. N'four was content.

It is, indeed, ironic that we know so much about the Cameroonian Mr. N'four, without knowing if he is a grunter or not. The Cameroonian Mr. N'four remains, in our minds, a real person with a real life; flesh and blood in cinema-scope. The Mr. N'four, our hotel neighbor, remains the grunter; a shadow, an enigma.

The Edifice and the Myth

HE LOOKED UP AND it seemed to merge with the heavens. The building, though by no means what one would call a skyscraper, swept up, its mirrored facade reflecting the cottony clouds; like a sideways ski jump that could hurl its rider to the stratosphere. He felt a lump in his throat as he imagined walking though those massive doors with the polished brass handles. This was so unexpected. He had never thought, never even dreamed, it could happen. As a simple and nearly invisible person, by some quirk of fate he had been chosen to work inside this edifice, inside this firm: a global power broker whose decisions impacted on the powerful and the weak around the world. Indeed, the firm was so awe-inspiring that it was commonly referred to only as "*the Organization*".

He was not a native of this western country that hosted the Organization. He grew up in the tropics, in a typical farming village where the major concerns were the coming rains and whether or not the teachers would be paid so that school could start. To him, it was a good life and he always thought he would, as his father before him, gain a modest education and then spend his time tilling the soil and looking after the family's livestock. He had no greater expectations.

However, as all knew, the fates can appear at any time and act in any way. Certainly it was more the fates than driving personal ambition or family zeal that guided his youthful pathway.

He managed to complete studies in the village school and, to all's surprise, none more than his own, he excelled. It was almost as though he had a natural attribute for academics; perhaps a trade-off for his obvious lack of natural ability in athletics. He found he was an exceptionally quick learner with a memory to match. So, diploma in hand, he was taken aback to find himself not joining his family's farm, but going off to the provincial capital to continue his education, thanks to a generous scholarship arranged by the principal of the village school and endorsed by the headman.

His acumen appeared to only sharpen and enhance his skills; as he moved through his studies, reaching higher and higher levels. It was almost a shock, and certainly unexpected, when he finally emerged from his journey with a doctorate in economics, finishing top of his class.

Much as this lofty status was unanticipated, it was also unclear to him where it would lead. For over a decade, day in and day out, he had set about his studies. They had at times been interesting and occasionally challenging, but education had turned into his career and it was the to and fro to the classroom that was the cadence of his life. He had no vision beyond the next exam. He had no plans beyond the next research topic. He had no life beyond school. Academia had become his comfort zone and he now had to peek outside to see what the real world offered.

He had always been brave and willing to enter the unknown. So, with a lump in his throat, he discarded his student garb and gingerly set foot on the sidewalks of his country's financial capital to discover what doors would open for a kid from the village with a PhD.

Having no specific hopes, he was not easily disappointed. He visited offices, asked advice, filled forms, and distributed résumés. He went round and round until his feet hurt. He took note of unenthusiastic "maybe's" as well as those replies that started "sorry, but in today's economy . . . ". He had no anxiety because he had no assumptions. He had foreseen nothing, so was not surprised when this is what he obtained. For him, this was a ritual; going through the motions that were expected. And when his savings expired, he packed his small bag and took a bus back to the village. After all, he had always thought he would be a farmer.

He was readily welcomed back into the village fold and in no time had begun the daily routine of caring for crops and animals. He shared a room with his brother in his father's house, but his family already spoke of marriage and of his building his own home on a lot not far off, close to the stream; a prime place for a young educated man to start a family.

In the evening, after the animals were fed and the evening meal taken, he and his father would sit and dare to dream of how this new life would be. How the new house would be built. What fields he would take as his own. Even what crops would be best given the current weather and market situation. Together they would chart the pathway for this educated young man, who might even one day become the village headman.

Then, one evening as they were so engrossed, as the wind whined outside announcing the arrival of a late-season thunder storm, there was a knock at the door. Leaving his farther to enjoy his after dinner coffee, he went to the door and upon opening it, to his astonishment, found a courier from the Post on the stoop; the hour for mail delivery having long past. But this messenger had no regular letter, he had an express envelope bedecked with bright red and blue stripes to denote its importance.

He and his father huddled over the envelope as they opened it, like children anxiously opening a Christmas present. In fact, this seemed to be a Christmas present and much more. Upon inspection, it was an invitation to return to the capital and have an interview for an economist position at a leading developmental agency: The Organization.

The announcement had been delayed by the rural mail system and the date was nearly upon them. Thus, early the next morning he packed his best coat and tie and boarded the bus.

A scant seventy-two hours later he was again on the bus, this time returning to the village. The interview had gone well. The questions had been simply answered. The interviewer, having a convivial demeanor, made it easy to relax. The morning after the consultation, he had been called by the assistant to the Organization's local Representative, who announced that he had been selected for the job. If he chose to accept, he needed to be at the Organization's Headquarters in one week's time. So now he was going back to the village to tell all that he would again be leaving.

That he would not be building his new house. That he would not be starting a family. That he would no longer be a farmer.

Departing is never easy and this time it was particularly difficult. He had no idea for how long he would be gone. His parents were getting up in years and he was unsure how, or if, he would find them when he next returned. His aunts, uncles, and senior cousins—all were aging. All were following more traditional lives. His friends, too, were establishing their own homes; lives that focused on the village and the farm. Lives that would soon be foreign to him. He wondered why he was sacrificing all that was known today for an unknown tomorrow?

He really knew very little about the job ahead of him. An offer from the Organization was seen as such a prestigious happenstance that few could even consider turning it down. The salary, the benefits, the duration, all were unclear. But it was the Organization. It had to be good, under any circumstances.

So now he looked up at the edifice that was the Organization. He strode bravely forward and firmly grasped the shining brass door handle. He was inside.

That had been then—the beginning. Now he was not only inside but an insider. He had initially undergone an exasperating year of trial and tribulation. The learning curve had been very steep. His fine academic record apart, this was a totally different culture, and as far away from the village as one could get. This was a universe dominated by bureaucrats, technocrats, administrators, and politicians who spoke a whole new language with many multi-syllable words. This was a domain dominated by rules and regulations that were bent to fit every situation, but were rarely wholeheartedly applied. This was a milieu where there were layers upon layers of authority intertwined with the ever changing guidelines; such that one had to always be careful—watching where you stepped and where you sat. But, this was the Organization.

He had to learn, unlearn, and relearn the dictums. He had to relearn the alphabet to accommodate all the new acronyms. He had to constantly forge new alliances to keep ahead of the changing political winds. He had to learn how to work in a tiny office shared by another economist.

Little had he realized that the position of economist was but one rung on a very long ladder, and a bottom rung at that. The Organization had scores of economists; senior economists, junior economists, resource economists, financial economists, rural development economists, environmental economists, agricultural economists, commodity and trade economists, even nutrition economists. There were economists on all fifteen floors of the edifice, as well as in the 12 department, 56 divisions, 27 special services, 64 task forces, and 23 select committees that occupied this space.

No one knew he had been a good student and no one cared. No one knew of his village, and, more importantly, no one cared he had been a farmer. Few even knew him as an individual, most saw him as a cog in a very complex and expensive machine. His greatest value seemed to be what level of visibility and prowess he could bring to his supervisors and senior colleagues. His good ideas became theirs, his proposals theirs, and, most of all, his solutions theirs. Intellectual property rights had nothing to do with intellect, as he was learning, but only with power; if you had the power, you had the rights.

This is not to paint a totally negative or even corrupt image of the Organization. All the adversities, and perhaps some of the realities, which confronted him were balanced by the rarified professional heights at which he found himself. The Organization had *la crème de la crème*. This was just possibly the greatest concentration of professionals to be found anywhere; specialists and experts in scores of fields—true world leaders in their disciplines.

It would take his breath away to walk down the maze of corridors, infused with energy, side stepping curriers with carts overloaded with documents, and interns with clipboards full of notes. When he read the name plates of the senior officers, it was a "who's who" in any of the multitude of scientific arenas where the Organization was the global center of excellence. These were men and women of great renown. People who had written the definitive texts. People who had done the pioneering work. People who had forgotten more than he could ever hope to know.

This was the majesty and the mastery of the Organization. Over decades, starting in those splintery years after the Second World War, it had created a culture and a niche for itself: a unique distinction as being the paramount agency in its field, staffed with the most preeminent specialists in the world. An institution above all others; a celebrity due chiefly to its unique and highly qualified world-class staff.

He knew egos were fragile things. This congregation of greatness was filled with self-esteem and one dared not shatter the delicate shells of self-admiration. So, he donned a cloak of simplicity; almost a mask of a country bumpkin. He became timid and respectful to all. He worked long hours. He attended endless meetings. He submitted the proper forms in triplicate. He wrote succinct reports. He developed a personal network of both those to help, and those who could help. Like a fluke entering the foot, he slowly, methodically but persistently moved up.

The suffocating interpersonal politics were countered with opportunities to take his work to the field. These trips were pure joy. He felt he was going back to his roots when he visited farms around the world; helping farmers do more to get more. He was in his element.

The years blended together and he was soon spouting the corporate jargon with the ease of an old timer. He now understood the intricacies of the administrative and bureaucratic webs that entangled the institution. It was still as unfriendly as always, still as incomprehensible; but he now knew his way around and through it well enough to where it was not an obstacle.

Budgets shrank. Staff were restructured. Programs were realigned. Priorities changed. Through these transformations, he continued to rise in the ranks; more so as the patriarchs retired. Soon he was a senior officer and sitting in one of the luxurious offices reserved for those of his illustrious rank.

But this ascent in status, welcome as it was, could not compensate for the accompanying, seemingly unavoidable loss of field time. Shifting responsibilities and greatly reduced budgets meant less travel, fewer projects, and less time on the ground. The resulting increased office time was frustratingly filled by meeting after meeting after meeting. He thought the Organization should change its logo, calling itself "home of the meeting people".

He felt the Organization was slipping off a muddy cliff. The more the financial crunch worsened, the more the bosses tried to adjust by following the latest *en vogue* concept while, of necessity, neglecting the core principles that had led them to greatness. It became a merry-go-round with a different pony being the flavor of each successive week, while the motor running the machine groaned, turning slower, and slower due to inattention. To add to the conundrum, as the ineffectiveness and inefficiencies of chasing rainbows became clearer and clearer, not only in-house, but also to clients; management tried to counter criticism by putting in place new systems and processes, ostensibly to address the problems, but in fact, to add to them.

The Organization had become an overloaded train. Overloaded with archaic and unnecessary bureaucracy. Overloaded with its own culture. Overloaded with its history. An overloaded train heading at top speed to a trestle that could not carry its weight. Frantically, the economist, like an engineer sought a solution. If the speed could not be reduced and the load lightened, the train would certainly fall to its death.

He slowly understood the process; like latex slowly filling the cup affixed to a *Hevea* tree. He began to feel the changes when it was too late. He had to accept them, be it unwillingly. He found himself now as one of the senior scientists: the post to which he had aspired, but for which he had held little hope of achieving. Yet, in spite of all, here he was, a senior officer in charge of an entire service.

This was his crowning glory. He was finally able to weave his personal, academic, and on-the-ground experiences into a tapestry that was genuinely impressive to behold. He had accolades, kudos, and certificates of merit. He was a professional in the truest sense.

He wanted to be good at what he did. He wanted to share the benefits of this knowledge with those who could most benefit from it. He wanted to make a difference.

However, he was not an idealist. His origins in the village had presented him with reality; with nearly too much evidence as to the nature of the human character. He had seen skullduggery and malfeasance. He had seen the powerful preying on the vulnerable. He had seen personal greed taking over the common good. He had seen and experienced these things in the village, in schools, and now in the Organization. But, in spite of this strong dose of reality, he remained an optimist, if a pragmatist. He honestly felt he could make a difference.

His ascendency to the head of a service now offered him the chance to put his hopes into practice. The opportunity to muster his skills, and build a program that could deliver real results. He now had the rare occasion to turn thoughts into deed. And, he took advantage of this moment. He designed a program that was innovative; that addressed the needs of the present, not anchored to the failures of the past. His approaches were pioneering, even revolutionary.

But, with difficult and Spartan times, the Organization spiraled out of control. What had been done could no longer be done. It became clear many of his plans would never leave his office. Yesterday's great idea became today's dust on the shelf. This was not due to any decrease in intrinsic value. Nevertheless, many of the best innovations would never see the light of day.

Desperately, he continued to struggle. Good work must somehow solicit good reactions. Somewhere, somehow these innovations must be able to be implemented. People would not just let such important work die. But, slowly the truth materialized, like a phantom from the fog. All his efforts could indeed lead to nothing.

Strangely, he learned, nothing was not failure. The Organization never failed. Like a chameleon, it would change its color. Like an amoeba, it would change its shape. But it did not fail: it progressed.

The fact that the edifice, that was once the global leader, was turning into an empty shell, was in fact not a fact. It was not even a thought nor a possibility. It was not mentioned. The Organization remained The Organization. It retained its global preeminence—at least in its own eyes. Nothing was forever and the changes in The Organization were simply signs of the times; it was growing and adapting to the twenty-first century.

At last, he saw the truth. Verifiable results were nice. Attaining goals was good. Making improvements was laudable. But, the facts remained the facts. The corporation was always right.

He carefully filed all his plans. Cleaned his drawing board. Freed his agenda. Became again a small cog in a very big machine.

He needed to rethink.

He was still a senior officer. He had his spacious office with a view of the city from the sixth floor. He had a budget, although seriously reduced. There was a great big world out there. However, this was not his former world. This had nothing to do with the farmer. This had nothing to do with practical, hands-on work. This was all about policies and practices; smoke and mirrors. This was about picking the low-hanging fruit: selecting a highly visible and politicized topic, organizing a global panel of experts to review its implications, and then writing a slick color report in five languages to repeat what farmers' associations had said fifteen years earlier. This was about quickly spending money, so that one could quickly ask for more. This was about using the press and social media to be at the forefront of the TV screen, if not of the farmer and urbanite in the developing world.

Thus, he spent his last years in the Organization attending meetings, sitting on august panels, and writing colorful reports. Inexplicably, he traveled even more than before. But these were lightening trips. Two- or three-day meetings with no forays into the hinterland. Two days to sit in air conditioned meeting rooms that all looked alike, talking to faceless groups that all resembled each other, eating from the same buffets the world-around. Each trip, however, led him closer to his target: retirement.

When retirement day finally came, he wanted no fanfare. Typically, there were cosmetic parties to thank the retiree for years of service. To thank them for their contribution. To thank them for having the perseverance to be able to survive until retirement. But he desperately wanted no such plastic *aurevoirs*. He was not leaving on top of his game. He was not, as he had once hoped, leaving, having passed on to his successor a successful and vibrant program active at the grassroots. He was simply leaving because the bell had rung, just as it had so many years ago when he had left the village school. There was nothing to celebrate. It was quite simply time to go home.

This time there was no bus. He drove into his village in a shiny new sedan that raised the eye brows of many villagers. This was not his first return since he left to joint the Organization. But his visits had become increasingly infrequent and he became increasingly distant.

He had tried to keep his roots well fertilized. He had initially come home every year. He stayed with his parents and had spent his days renewing acquaintances among family and friends. He had even bought the lot by the stream and built a home.

Yet, as the years progressed, his parents' health deteriorated and they finally passed away. His aunts and uncles now were also gone. His childhood friends became strangers. He felt less and less part of the community. He became an infrequent visitor, generally only staying a few nights in his house and then going to the provincial capital, where he had a sumptuous flat.

This time, his arrival in the village was not to start his new life of retirement at his old home, but rather to delicately and finally extract himself. He knew he would never again be a farmer. He would never again sit quietly on the mat as the headman and elders decided who should farm the lowlands, and who would till the hillsides. He could no longer be content to live without electricity, not to mention Internet. He was no longer of the village.

Having remained unmarried and childless, with always the improbable idea in the back of his mind that he would one day return to the village, to settle in his house by the stream and start his family, he had devoted his efforts elsewhere and now found himself a retiree alone.

He gave his house to his brother's younger son and divided his fields among his brother and sister. He paid his respects to the headman. He invited all his extended family to the village square for roast chicken and beer. He then drove down the dusty road in his shiny car, back to his flat in the city.

He painstakingly forged a new life in the city. He had a plan. He would call on all of his many contacts from the Origination and establish a group, a cabinet of experts, who would be able to do what the Organization no longer chose to do. A group that would be able to provide the real services people expected. A group that would have the expertise and know-how to get the job done in the village and in the community. A group that would allow him to do what he had not been able to do. A group that would reconnect him with his own village. A group that would make a difference.

He engaged a lawyer to assist in establishing a formal mandate for this group. He carefully crafted a vision statement along with the accompanying goals and objectives. He methodically listed all the world-class experts he could enroll. He meticulously wrote a letter to each, describing what he was planning and how he hoped to accomplish his aims. To each he sent this notice by express courier, much like the missive he had received, that had so changed his life; what now seemed like a lifetime ago.

He then waited for the replies from these colleagues, the world's top experts. The people who could make a difference. He waited and he waited. No replies came. No one cared.

Thinking Back Looking Forward

IT MAY WELL BE amazing. I can still vividly see the images. I grew up in what would probably pass for middle America on the West Coast. We had what was a self-contained town in the 50s. There was Carter's Grocery that even offered home delivery back in those days. There was Busman's Feed and Seed that did sell a few scraggly aquarium fish and pet supplies in addition to the promised feed and seed. There was Bell's Hardware that really only sold hardware including rows of different nails in metal bins that you bought by the pound. There was Shaw's Stationary that sold all kinds of papers, pens, and inks, the store having a unique aroma like an old mimeograph machine or an office not used too much. There was even Hal's Sporting Goods that sold a whole bunch of gear for school sports, hunting, and fishing; including canvas tennis shoes and bamboo fishing poles. In spite of all the paraphernalia, the shop always seemed to smell of gun oil, perhaps a result of Mr. Hal's love affair with hunting, proudly displaying freshly shot pheasants, ducks, and geese hanging out by the front door each season. Interestingly, none of these places offered or served coffee, accepted credit cards, nor had noise-making security grids at the store's entrance.

I remember going to the mill which was infused with the pungent spice of caustic dipping tank chemicals. It would be a real treat to have a nickel to use in the candy machines; white metal rectangles on the wall with a kind of rotating belt with shelves full of candy—after twisting the knob to move the belt to the morsel of your choice, you lined the bar up in the window, put in the 5¢, pushed down the lever, and picked your tasty delight out of the box at the bottom. Pop machines were almost as sophisticated. The short-necked glass bottles were hanging from a set of metal slots, like so many deer hung out by an old-time hunter, in the days when wildlife seemed to be limitless. The bottles dangled in cold water like a kid sitting on the edge of a dock on a high mountain lake. You would have to jiggle and finesse the bottles around the slots like one of those old alphabet pocket games until you could slide it into a kind of hopper with a metal tongue that would release when you deposited your 10¢. It was rumored that one could forego all the gymnastics and save his dime by popping off the cap right in the slots and draining the contents with a straw supplied by the drinker.

Yep, those were the days. My buddy just reminded me of how, back then, his Mother would drive around town to find gas for 24.9¢ a gallon; and for that astounding amount you got your windshield cleaned, oil and tires checked, and even sometimes a free dinner plate or coffee cup, not to mention Gold Bond or Green stamps. At home, you were visited by the Fuller Brush Man and the Milkman, who brought milk in glass bottles along with other dairy products; and even big cardboard boxes, filled with laundry powder, with a kitchen glass buried deep inside. The dry cleaner delivered your clean clothes and doctors made house-calls.

This was not life emulating art. This was the lifestyle that was the object of the TV shows of the period; *Leave it to Beaver* or *Father Knows Best*. It was a Norman Rockwell vision of post war near perfection. This was reality growing up in the 50s.

Today I receive those e-mail chain letters saying, if you can remember penny candy, baseball cards in bubble gum, PF Fliers, and all sorts of other esoteric things, then you must be over 50. I can and I am.

I now try to look back at this rosy childhood, like a time traveler looking into a time machine or the Ghost of Christmas Past baring old truths. Was it utopia, or is this just selective memory?

Over four decades ago I left the byways of small-town America and went to Central Africa in what turned out to be the beginning of a professional career as a stranger in a strange land. Over the years I do hope I developed a sensitivity for local life and customs.

Growing up in a small tropical village composed of several score of mud-block homes interspersed with mango and avocado trees along with coffee and plantain fields, may seem light-years away from Carter's, Busman's and Bell's. A community overseen by a traditional chief may appear to be the antithesis of a town run by a mayor [who I never saw nor even knew his name]. Kids wearing Levis and Converse may seem to be from a different planet when compared to school-goers wearing used clothes that come in bales to the village market that is every eight days; and who go to school either barefoot or wearing flip-flops, that have been overhauled so many times the spongy sole is nearly worn through. These students, gleefully, going to woebegone school "sheds" along the shaded village paths; paths lined with flowers and small vegetable patches. The air filled with the essence of wood-smoke from open hearths, goat manure, and an omnipresent inhalant of fine red dust; except during the coffee blooming season, when the air is perfumed with a truly delectable and indescribable bouquet.

It is amazing that those who grew up in this and similar tropical villages in the 50s often refer to that time as *l'époque d'or*—the Golden Period. There are not e-mails listing all the minutiae of the time, but there is, nonetheless, deep nostalgia.

Two different worlds that are part and parcel of my world.

So, I also try to touch the Ghost of Christmas Past's cloak and look back and in at these times in another land, with another people; and see how they relate to the lives of Beaver, June, Wally, and Ward Cleaver. Was the Golden Period utopia, or is this just selective memory?

I struggle with the answer to this question for the two worlds in my life. What is clear is that everyone in both worlds, from the pandering politicians to the harassed heads of households, thinks these yesteryears were truly close to perfection.

Certainly the recent declining economic conditions of the populace in both worlds contribute to this rosy view of the past. It is tough to get by today. Just like the demise of my 5¢ chocolate bar or 10¢ Coke, folks in Central Africa have seen what little they have become less and less. Those years ago, when I first arrived to learn the redolence of cassava and the cry of the crowned crane, a middle class family of town folks could go to market and get a full weeks supply of top quality food for less than $15; today this would buy only a few kilos of meat and rice. In the rural areas in those days, a day laborer would make about $1; today, common laborers on farms and similar enterprises, are compensated with about 80¢ a day.

Times gone by do look good today and our politicians are quick to remind us that they are the ones who can reinstate the old-time family values and reinvigorate the economy. It seems we are encouraged to look back to move forward.

But, as I grasp the Ghost's cloak, I too am like Ebenezer when he was warned by his deceased partner Marley to think more of his fellow man. Putting politics and economics aside for the moment, what of people?

I can emphatically say that folks in Central Africa and the western US are not that different. While it may seem as though there are two worlds, these are inhabited by one people. These people feel their society has metamorphosed from a kinder, gentler community of yore to a dog-eat-dog milieu of the present. While the latter may be true, is the former really the case: were we kinder and gentler?

I tend to think not. While, as all of us, I can only look at my own personal experiences as being the sole absolutes, with which I have had direct contact. If I can believe my senses, I tend to think these experiences, while reinforcing the oneness of humanity, do cast doubt on the kinder and gentler nature of this humanity.

I recall often the unexpected deaths of friends or acquaintances in Central Africa that were attributed to poisoning. While I suspect today many of these were no more than undiagnosed but serious medical problems. In the absence of accepted knowledge to the contrary, the assumption was that the person had been poisoned and that, more times than not, the poisoning was due to jealousies.

Speaking of jealousies, I also recall visiting a group of farmers that had won a contest for applying good farming practices. The prize was metal roofing sheets to replace their thatched roofs.

However, at my arrival, the roofing sheets were carefully stored in a back room and not on the roof. Why? The prize-winners were afraid of arousing jealousies among others in the village when they assumed such a visible sign of wealth, as having metal roofs. Having more, or simply having the appearance of having more, seems to be adequate stimulus to overcome the kinder and gentler attributes, reverting to baser instincts.

This would also often seem to be the case when there have been altercations in areas receiving large numbers of refugees. To the casual observer, these may seem to be conflicts between indigenous or local populations; nothing new in the annals of human history. However, although xenophobia may be a factor, in those cases I have encountered, the real match that lit the flame was the issue of wealth or perceived wealth.

The refugee camps were self-contained units with their own schools, health centers, and other facilities. The staff manning these were paid by the various organizations that supported the camps, and they were paid. Outside the camp perimeters, there was a daily life for local people which also included education, clinics, and other public service providers. But, local civil servants were infrequently and totally inadequately paid. The problem, therefore, was the disparities in treatment of service providers within and outside the camps. The need and suffering of the refugees completely overshadowed, by perceived and, more than likely, real inequities among equals.

So, if we think these anomalies relate only to those in Africa, we should hold tightly to the Ghost's cloak and visit the well-known phenomena of "keeping up with the Jones's". While the farmers wished to avoid misunderstandings by keeping the playing field level, the United States' West Coast can be filled with the in-your-face chant: "I'm better than you are!" From the biggest house and most expensive automobile right down to the most extravagant holiday decorations. It seems as though people are determined to demonstrate they are better than their neighbors, to the inevitable deterioration of any hoped-for brotherhood.

Thus, thinking back as I try to look forward, I release the Ghost's cloak and resign myself to the fact that there really were not kinder nor gentler times gone by and that there is really no need to think about "returning" to family values. As humans, we are endowed with a spectrum of emotions, amongst which jealousy can be paramount. It is in the interests of our own sense of being, as well as in the interests of those who look to us as role models, to try and keep this native emotion at bay. No one will ever have everything and the less we fixate on what others have and the more we try to be open-minded and cordial to those with whom we share our personal space, the more we will enhance our society and truly lay the groundwork for enduring social values.

From the despots mismanaging governments to the kings of industry and technology, we have daily contact with those who are already so wealthy, that they do not know what to do with all their riches. Nevertheless, this immoral excess does, in no way, prevent them from the self-indulgence of aggressively trying to get more and more. If unfettered, there will be no end.

There certainly was not a utopia in the days of my youth. Although life was perhaps simpler and less instantaneous communications provided more needed breathing space. This is, moreover, not a case of universal selective memory. Some may honestly be wrapped in nostalgia, to the point of not being able to see the present for the past, but most are likely using the past as a transparent shield, like those used by riot police. You can clearly see through it, but it deflects any undesirable or unpleasant missiles. It dulls the pain of today with the anesthesia of fond memories of yesterday.

We are not studiously holding up the past to measure the present, although perhaps we should. We are not, or at least most of us, suggesting reinstating segregation or apartheid or going back to polio along with endemic measles. As baby-boomers, we are perhaps collectively morose about our aging bodies and maybe just a little intimidated by a future we do not fully understand. Our security blanket is our past which is warm and comfortable and known. Whether in Central Africa or on the West Coast, it is easier to look backward to think forward.

The Moons' Glow

AT TIMES, THE DIAGNOSIS of the situation may seem overly harsh, as my fraternal twin lunar worlds often force very septic views of each other; the realities of one insist on an honest appraisal of the other. It is very much like someone criticizing his neighbor's yard, viewing it across the across the hedge without really knowing why it is as it is.

However, in my case, much of the time my two moons are on different circuits, like a change-over switch to the mains for the generator. I find myself in one place or the other and have the switch set to the moon that corresponds to the right place at the right time. Recently though, it was as though I had a short circuit; my wires crossed. The switch was set on there when I was here, and my moons collided.

Being able to set the switch to the right position was at the very least a coping strategy, and maybe a cop-out. For, when the switch and the moon were synchronized, I was in the one place living the one life, completely oblivious to the other place and the other life. This conveniently allowed for selective memory and discerning action, picking and choosing what baggage I wished to carry, just as when I prepared to fly back and forth across the Atlantic and got my suitcase ready.

But this time I packed badly and found myself out of sync. I was back living in the land of my parents, the land where I had grown up and gone to school, but I was a stranger. Although I had made the transition scores of times before, it was like when someone in those 1960 sci-fi shows got their molecules scrambled by the transporter during an otherwise routine "beaming", somewhere deep inside my physiology and/or psychology had hit a glitch in the transport and I was not able to make the seamless and painless transition.

Perhaps it was because this time it was indeed an extended stay in my home of record while the medical profession tried to redress years of abuse. Perhaps it was this redress or this abuse that led to the problem. For whatever reason, for the first time in years I looked around and began to ask "why?"

I wasn't just on home-leave to go to the dentist and get my supply of State-side stuff I couldn't get elsewhere. I was seeing things and wondering: why isn't there any news on the news; why do people proudly pierce and cut their skin; why are the rich so rich and why are there so many who are not; why do people live plastic lives that never were; why do people not care?

As a youngster I had an electric train. My Dad had really done a terrific job of laying out a whole world on a single sheet of plywood and my train would choo-choo through plastic villages, with plastic houses, plastic trees, and plastic dogs. When my reality switch did not switch, I felt I was living in one of the villages serviced by my electric train. I would walk with our dog around the neighborhood and see lots of make-believe Brownstones interspersed with make-believe European-like cafés and Asianesque tea houses. The houses looked like great fields of mushrooms, one looking like the other—one place declared triumphantly they offered eighteen different floor plans—probably all within the same size box.

I don't know if these are officially referred to as apartments, flats, condominiums, duplexes, or townhouses. Whatever the term, they are not that far away from my train set. They have plastic siding, plastic fittings, plastic sashes and doors, with plastic chairs and tables on their mini patios. In front of these poorly hung plastic doors are all variety of luxury cars and SUVs. It is rumored they even sell mud in a spray can so these urban villagers can spray their cars on Sunday, pretending they had been in the bush when they go back to work on Monday.

Some of the folks behind the wheels of these fine motorcars have tattoos on their buttocks caressing the leather seats, tattoos on the forearm, studs in the ear, lip, and cheek, red or green hair and clothes that look like they came from the *frippery* (stalls selling used clothing) in an African market. In fact, in many ways, the folks so adorned look almost other-worldly, more alien than those who actually come from what many consider as other worlds.

Moreover, as language is often one of the emblems of being foreign, while few Americans speak what would be considered the Queen's English, I am truly flabbergasted at what passes for the English language today. Seemingly to add insult to injury, the politicians argue about the need for only one national language when all in fact speak no true language, if a language implies following basic rules of grammar and usage. From the TV announcers and reality show hosts to the burger flipper, it's "me and my friend", "I'm good", and "where you at" not to mention a plethora of terms like "bling" and "booty" that add to the mishmash of the US pidgin apparently *en vogue*.

So, am I a stranger in a strange land?

I suppose the short answer is yes. When I hear of the threat posed by immigrants from those who live in a country based on immigrants and a country run by those who have made their riches on the backs of immigrants, I fear I am in the wrong place. When I hear that a wrong war is right, that imperialism is correct, and that might is right, I do wonder if I am where there was a war of Independence in 1776. When religions are equated with terror while, at the same time, religious extremists vie for power in the same government that condemns other religions, I see how shallow our roots have become. When hypocrisy reigns, I look in vain for the truth. It is not my switch and my moons that are out of sync; I am now out of sync.

Or am I?

I think back to the dark smoke-filled bars of the mill town of my birth where I first learned to really like the tart taste of beer; establishments filled with loggers, farmers, and shoe salesmen. As we chain-smoked and gulped far too many pitchers, the conversations ultimately settled on family; how kids were doing in school, if someone was sick, or someone else was planning a fishing trip, if grocery or gas prices were rising, or if the local high school football team was losing. Bouquets of the banalities of life, the things that really mattered.

Some years later, when sitting in a Central African palm wine house during market day in dry season when the cool wine tasted like ambrosia to dust-encrusted lips, the folks gathered around the wobbly table, downing glass after glass of the milky liquid, talked with growing decibels of their priorities: keeping kids in school, healing the ill, having good harvests, visiting far-off family members, and supporting the local football [soccer] team.

Two moons inextricably linked to one planet.

Verse

Two Worlds

Two worlds, each with a part, neither with the whole.

Two worlds, far apart in distance, close in humanity.

Two worlds, one person, one life.

The Two

Lives so different, yet so much the same.

Lives touching, but difficult to touch.

Lives that can merge, making a stronger union.

Faded Images

I lie awake,

Eyes closed, I stare into the darkness,

I listen to the silence.

Yesterdays unroll like a dusty tapestry,

The images faded, the odor stale.

Grasslands

The soft blue sky embraces the breeze

That ruffles the elephant grass like a petty-coat going
    down stairs,

Puffs of dust ride the wind, stuffing the nose like chalk
  dust.

A kite circles slowly, riding the drafts, eyeing the field
  mouse burrow.

A sun bird flirts from tough stem to tough stem, looking
  for nectar, but finding little.

A scent of wood smoke is in the air, as the wind carries
  the cries of a child and the yelp of a dog.

The horizon shimmers, like ripples in a still pool.

The grasslands settle into the rhythm of high noon.

The Rondaval

Ducking inside, there's a dusty carbony smell you can
  almost taste.

Small shafts of light cut the darkness like headlights on a
  lonely night road.

The floor of packed earth is soft and clean under foot.

The sound of bare feet scuffing over the bare surface
  bounces off the adobe walls.

Outside there are echoes from a well-lit world.

Inside there is a warmth that is not man-made.

Eyes

Eyes with a twinkle of wisdom,

a flash of knowing.

An understanding of futility and reward.

Eyes, hidden behind half-closed lids.

Eyes, under a dark and weathered brow.

Eyes that belie the impoverished body.

Eyes to the future.

The Market

Pigs screaming. Goats laughing.

People joining the song at all octaves, in scores of
languages.

Pots banging, horns blaring, bicycle bells clanging.

Trucks and fires smoking, crucibles steaming, meat
grilling.

The tart smell of new fabric, the tang of cassava and the
sweetness of palm oil

merge with the pungency of urine and rotting vegetables.

Herds of humanity throb and surge left and right.

The market comes alive.

Accra morning

The predawn sky a plum,

puce with a fringe of pink.

The call from the minaret mixing with the call of the
lone rook and the crow of the neighborhood rooster.

The scent of frangipani mingling with the drains chan-
neling humanities' waste combine on the morning
breeze that rattles the banana leaves and palm fronds.

A not-so-far-off truck complains about being out and
about so early, while the first flights circle the airport.

The mêlée of today begins.

www.ingramcontent.com/pod-product-compliance
Lightning Source LLC
Chambersburg PA
CBHW051144020726
47501CB00005B/1665